Education and Intercultural Identity

Education and Intercultural Identity offers a dialogue between influential authors Zygmunt Bauman and Agostino Portera that reflects on and discusses contemporary events and issues relating to the crisis of global normativity, education and intercultural identity.

Centred around a previously unpublished dialogue between Bauman and Portera, the book contains an extended introduction by Riccardo Mazzeo that traces key themes in the dialogue and highlights the importance of education in our globalized world. The book highlights that intercultural and multicultural education are the best developed models to meet modern-day challenges that include religious pluralism, pollution and conflict. It also contains timely material relating to significant issues affecting society today, including the refugee crisis, rising authoritarian nationalism, and the risks and challenges of globalization and sustainability.

This book will be of great interest for academics, scholars and students in the fields of intercultural and multicultural education, sociology and the sociology of education.

Zygmunt Bauman has been one of the most influent sociologists of the last century and of the first two decades of the present century. Among his dozens of books are *Modernity and the Holocaust* and *Liquid Modernity*.

Agostino Portera is professor at the University of Verona, Italy and visiting professor all over the world. As a prominent expert of intercultural studies he has published many books in Italian and English.

Riccardo Mazzeo is an editor, an essayist and a translator. His published books include *On Education* and *In Praise of Literature* with Zygmunt Bauman.

Education and Intercultural Identity

A Dialogue between Zygmunt
Bauman and Agostino Portera

**Zygmunt Bauman and
Agostino Portera
Edited and introduced by
Riccardo Mazzeo**

Routledge
Taylor & Francis Group

LONDON AND NEW YORK

First published 2021
by Routledge
2 Park Square, Milton Park, Abingdon, Oxon OX14 4RN

and by Routledge
605 Third Avenue, New York, NY 10158

Routledge is an imprint of the Taylor & Francis Group, an informa business.

© 2021 Zygmunt Bauman, Agostino Portera and Riccardo Mazzeo

The right of Zygmunt Bauman, Agostino Portera and Riccardo Mazzeo to be identified as author[/s] of this work has been asserted by him/her/them in accordance with sections 77 and 78 of the Copyright, Designs and Patents Act 1988.

British Library Cataloguing-in-Publication Data
A catalogue record for this book is available from the British Library

Library of Congress Cataloging-in-Publication Data
A catalog record has been requested for this book

ISBN: 978-0-367-64254-9 (hbk)
ISBN: 978-0-367-64256-3 (pbk)
ISBN: 978-1-003-12370-5 (ebk)

Typeset in Times New Roman
by MPS Limited, Dehradun

Contents

PART III
Conclusions   67
AGOSTINO PORTERA

Part I

Introduction

Introduction

Riccardo Mazzeo

Intercultural identity as a form of destiny

Bauman and Portera were born on the same day, 19 November, although many years apart.

My *maestro*, Bauman, was born in Poland. He fought during the war and was later exiled; after a brief period in Israel, where he was reluctantly forced to live after expatriation from his native country by expulsion order, with his wife and three children, and having no other place to go, he went to England, where he taught and wrote for almost half a century.

Portera, was born in Sicily in Porto Empedocle. He went to study, first in Rome, then in Germany, where he met his German companion and mother of his children, before his appointment at the University of Verona, where he holds seminars, master's courses and a range of other initiatives of various kinds.

He is constantly invited to speak at universities in many different countries, requests he is always delighted to accept. Like Bauman, he considers the exile or migrant status (intellectual, in his case) of the foreigner as a benediction and a privilege because it permits him to explore his own nature and that of the *Other*, in special depth, proximity, offline sharing; authentic and tangible; not only through cognition, but embodied.

Both authors are wonderfully successful examples of "intercultural identity".

They met in Verona in 2013, where Portera had organized an event on intercultural subjects involving 160 expert lecturers from every corner of the world. He had also invited Bauman and his second wife, Aleksandra Kania, along with me, so we could present the book that the *maestro* and I had written together, *On Education,*[1] held in the splendid Gran Guardia palazzo in Piazza Bra. Later he asked Bauman if he would agree to collaborate in writing a conversation-book on a topic with which he was very familiar: interculturalism and education. Bauman agreed and suggested that later, they would have asked me to write the introduction to their text.

Bauman died on 9 February 2017, before they had finished their work together; only four chapters had been completed, and we were all too sad at his loss to want to continue. The uncompleted work remained unfinished.

Recently, however, Portera asked whether I thought it might be a good idea to publish the text all the same; the exchanges are stimulating, sometimes even brilliant, and even though Portera has been published in several different countries, he placed the emphasis above all on the aspects that Bauman had written during their correspondence and that did not deserve to fall into obscurity. So, I asked the Bauman family if they would agree to publication, and having obtained their permission, I promised I would revise the text by December 2018 and would write the introduction that had been decided so that the book would be ready for publication.

Interculturalism, education, reciprocal fecundation and fertile hybridity were among Bauman's core topics; they deal with the exchanges and transfer of knowledge, not only among people, but also among disciplines. In the last book we wrote together, *In Praise of Literature*,[2] Bauman and I dealt with the compelling, decisive and imperative necessity to combine human sciences such as sociology, anthropology, psychology, etc, with literature, film-making, theatre and art in general. In the end, the corpus of both spheres covers only a part of the spectrum, and if we wish to hunt for the peep hole in the theatre curtain of objective experience (*Erfahrungen*) and subjective experience (*Erlebnisse*), objective research data and verifiable quantitative elements are not sufficient; we also need the transcendent aspects that only art can reveal.

In the conclusive chapter of his famous text *Liquid Modernity*,[3] which forms a kind of appendix, Bauman explains how the most succulent fruits of literature and human sciences were produced by authors who plunged with determination into the most diverse and pluralistic realities of interculturalism. Already, 200 years ago, Alfred de Musset launched his battle cry, "Great artists have no country", but 150 years later, Juan Goytisolo "probably the greatest among living Spanish writers" who, like Bauman, died in 2017, pointed out that when Spain accepted in the name of Catholic piety and under the influence of the Inquisition, a highly restrictive notion of national identity, the country became towards the end of the 16th century a "cultural desert".

Goytisolo wrote in Spanish but lived for many years in Paris and in the United States before settling in Morocco. No other Spanish writer has had so many works translated into Arabic. Goytisolo believed that the reason for his creativity lay in the plurality of his sources of inspiration. He stated that "Intimacy and distance create a privileged situation. Both are necessary", defining his native tongue as "the authentic homeland in his exile".

Another "intercultural" author mentioned by Bauman is Jacques Derrida, who, at the age of 12, was expelled from his lycée in Algeria in 1942, because of the anti-Semitic quotas imposed by the Vichy government, since he was Jewish. In the United States, he was considered French; however, in France, because of the slight Algerian accent that sometimes appeared in his refined eloquence as a professor at the Sorbonne, he was perceived as "foreign". Perhaps this was the reason that inspired his theory on the superiority of the written word over verbal speech. In any case, "Derrida was to remain 'stateless'. However, this did not mean having no cultural homeland. Quite the contrary: being 'culturally stateless' meant having more than one homeland, building a home of one's own on the crossroads between cultures; Derrida became and remained a *métèque,* a cultural hybrid. His 'home on the crossroads' was built of language".[4]

On the other hand, Musset felt that elevated art was not stateless, but had different homelands, with one perspective directed inwards and the other facing outwards, in this way managing to combine intimacy with detachment, just as George Steiner considered that Samuel Beckett, Jorge Luis Borges and Vladimir Nabokov had been able to feel "at home" in different linguistic worlds.

The dark and painful side of interculture

Bauman raised the status of the exile, the migrant, the stateless person, to a creative dimension that is invaluable for humanity: "One needs to live, to visit, to know intimately more than one such universe, to spy out human invention behind any universe's imposing and apparently indomitable structure",[5] with a very specific appendix: "To create (and so also to discover) always means breaking a rule; following a rule is mere routine, more of the same – not an act of creation. For the exile, breaking rules is not a matter of free choice, but an eventuality that cannot be avoided. Exiles do not know enough of the rules reigning in their country of arrival, nor do they treat them unctuously enough for their efforts to observe them and conform to be perceived as genuine and approved".[6] And this is where the current problems with migration begin.

The fundamental question lies in the fact that the two ways of immersing oneself in another world are essentially different: there is that of the *haves* (tourists and transnational entrepreneurs) and that of the *have nots* (all those who have had to flee hunger or war). The former are not forced to adapt themselves to the rules of the country where they arrive thanks to their sizeable credit cards that can procure interpreters, staff and mediators of every kind. It is far more difficult for the latter, who, although perfectly capable of expanding the cultural horizons of the local population in the country where they land, no longer have this option because of *retrotopia* and souverainism, which oppose globalization; they consider migrants simply as intruders, as contemptible and dangerous people to be expelled beyond their borders and made to disappear from view.

Bauman explains the logics of the war among the poor that arises between the lowest and the second-to-lowest in society, the local *have nots* (who have lost their jobs or who are impoverished and crushed by taxes, finding it a struggle to reach the end of the month) and the dispossessed migrants who land on our shores to escape starvation or death; in his explanation, he uses Aesop's fable of the hares and the frogs, in his book, *Strangers at Our Door:*

> The Hares of that tale were so persecuted by the other beasts that they did not know where to go. As soon as they saw even a single animal approach them, off they used to run. One day they saw a troop of wild Horses stampeding nearby and in a panic all the Hares scuttled off to a lake close by, determined to drown themselves rather than live in such a continual state of fear. But just as they got near the bank of the lake, a troop of Frogs, frightened in their turn by the approach of the Hares, scuttled off and jumped into the water. "Truly", said one of the Hares, "things are not as bad as they seem. No need to choose death over life in fear". The moral of Aesop's tale is straightforward: the satisfaction that this Hare felt – a welcome respite from the routine despondency of daily persecution – he has drawn from the revelation that there is always someone in a yet worse pickle than he himself.[7]

With the rise of globalization, government focus on the population has become clouded; in fact, it has almost eclipsed, and an increasing number of people have slipped into a vulnerable situation composed of dejected "hares". But now, we have seen the arrival of migrants who are in an even more desperate condition, deprived of any rights, even the most fundamental; this provides a source of gratification and offers a target for people to offload the blame for their own afflictions. The policies of politicians like Salvini, Le Pen, Orbán, etc., are not able to resolve global problems at local or national level, but they need the support of voters; so what better excuse than to direct their voters' personal fear against these "dangerous", "dirty" and "threatening" foreigners?

It is basically the same attitude as *white trash,* the white underclass in the Southern United States, who found consolation at the sight of *negroes,* so lacking in any ostensibly human characteristics that they were even deprived of white skin; a similar method was used by Trump, calling the workers of the *rust belt* to rejoice in the sealing of US borders to defend the country from the "dirty" *Latinos,* all violent drug traffickers. This attitude has corroborated the statement by Orbán that "all terrorists are migrants". Bauman wrote that many people feel that: "'immigrants pose health risks for the native population' (77%), 'immigrants substantially increase the danger of terrorist attacks' (77%)".[8]

Apart from the events that had influenced his life, Bauman's "intercultural identity" also formed tangible choices, something which was manifest when the University of Prague awarded him an honorary degree; it is customary to play the national anthem of the graduate, and Bauman was asked whether he preferred the Polish anthem (the country from which he had been expelled) or that of Great Britain (where he had been welcomed with every honour, but where he continued to feel himself an "immigrant"). He chose the Anthem of Europe, celebration of the brotherhood of man, elevated with the verses "Alle Menschen werden Brüder" (All people become brothers). That "werden/become" signals the importance of identity "as something that should be invented rather than discovered; like the aspired goal of some great effort, an objective, something that must be still constructed from square one, or chosen from alternative proposals".[9]

For Portera and Bauman a necessary and urgent way to face the above challenges is *education.* Both recognize the need of education in societies of the fluid modernity, where changes, opportunities and risks are paramount.

Portera in many publications[10] stated the necessity to invest in intercultural education. He considers intercultural education the best developed model given in the nowadays global, interdependent and multicultural world. The intercultural model is located between universalism and relativism, based on the advantages of transcultural and multicultural education, with the addition of the opportunity of encounter, dialogue and conflict management. Educators, teachers, politicians, journalists and all citizens should also assume intercultural competences,[11] for facing adequately and competently all conflicts and recognizing opportunities and risks related to the new situation.

Optimism and pessimism

Personally, I find almost moving the contrast between Portera's optimism, urging listeners to place emphasis on the positive aspects, opportunities and edifying consequences of the current situation, and Bauman's slightly raised eyebrow, that tended to affirm the more critical and sombre aspects. During Bauman's conferences, dozens of times I heard him asking these questions, and making similar calls and pleas. Something similar happened during the conference with Ágnes Heller,[12] when I was introducing Bauman: Heller sustained that beauty was essential in order to save the world, while Bauman argued that if we truly want to do something for the world in which we live, we need to draw attention to the negative aspects, the dangers, the changes and the reconstructions necessary. Although I am extremely fond of Heller and have enormous respect for her as an intellectual, in my introduction, I strongly supported Bauman's viewpoint: "I have no objections at all against beauty, but I consider that human beings can learn much more from dystopias and from being aware of the *evil* and the degeneracy that exist also in communities that consider themselves, and are considered, righteous, than from the magical snowy peaks of the Dolomites, the poetic beauty of early morning dew, or the *Déjeuner sur l'herbe by* Manet".[13]

For his part, Bauman insisted on the necessity of the artist or the sociologist to focus attention on those aspects of our deeply corrupt world that are allowed to remain unnoticed, and quoted an extract from an interview that Michael Haneke, the great philosopher and film maker, accorded to Elisabeth Day: "I recently returned to Austria after a trip abroad, and I saw news and headlines describing terrible events concerning earthquakes and explosions, but all this news was accompanied by pleasant cheerful music. Everything had been commercialised, and made attractive; it had been transformed into an entertainment program. This is where the danger lies: that we are no longer able to notice that terrible things like this are happening".

I wish to be perfectly clear: the role of Portera and Heller deserves all our respect. It is a perspective that is not contradictory, but is complementary to that of Bauman, a great educator and great philosopher, who at the age of 89, after being imprisoned by the Nazis and rebelling (continuing to the present day) against the arrogance of the Hungarian Government, enjoys life (exhibitions, fine books, essays, theatre, films, good food, travel) like few people today and has a perspective that is more than legitimate, and even compelling. The enthusiasm and pedagogical commitment of Portera in welcoming scholars or travelling around the world with his wonderful trusting smile: how can we possibly negate these bursts of vitality, able to nurture life and make it blossom in a blaze of light like the wound of Siddhartha?

However, Bauman is a sociologist, and in this book, he explains his position with absolute clarity: "It is the expanding intolerance to injustice that results in the expansion of justice". Therefore, if in "the 18th Century America, which we praise as the founder of modern democracy, rebellion against slavery was a violation of divine and/or natural order and a severely punishable crime", if "for the most enlightened and high-minded political leaders of the European 19th and early 20th century, keeping women out of the political body and out of public life was, again, a verdict of nature [...] to enlist people to the cause of justice, you need first to open their eyes to the injustices of the status quo".

We are all aware that each one of us has a different perception of events. In 50% of cases, our perceptions are mistaken, even in discussions with the people closest to us. But, for Bauman, in particular, there are "eucolon" dimensions (including "the occurrences he/she considers good and well") and "discolon" dimensions (focused "on what he/she found disparaging and off-putting"). And it is precisely for this reason that, as a sociologist, Bauman decided to place himself on the side of the "discolon".

Other strategies in life: from the sacred to the technological

In his latest book,[14] Mauro Magatti, a friend of mine and Bauman's, explains the transformation that occurred with the concept of the sacred and its inevitable consequences on religion.

The word "power" has two distinct interpretations: power (energy) must "emerge" in action, of which it is the driving force, and to become apparent, it must swerve away from what existed previously with "a beginning, a discontinuity". On the other hand, according to Simmel, power/potency, (influence/control) is the social form of power: it compresses, it shapes, it delineates, and it creates the profile that permits it to exist. At the same time, however, it does not contain it,

because power distances itself from any form of limitation; it is cen-
trifugal and irrepressible.

In the history of the world, power was born and became manifest in
the sacred. Confronted by a power from above that was all-
encompassing, man had no choice but to attribute it with a "numi-
nous" quality that existed outside and above mankind, and Habermas
defined rituals as the assemblage of actions that enabled man to establish a contact with the Divine. The repetition of ceremonial words
and gestures provided human beings with security, as man was dis-
oriented when confronted by the often intimidating mystery and ma-
jesty of the cosmos.

According to Girard, early Christianity possessed the quality of
inverting the "sacrificial logic" of the scapegoat, because while con-
serving His supreme nature, God was made man, humble and pow-
erless enough to allow Himself to be crucified. It is the concept of
incarnation, combining transcendence and immanence, that made this
religion so popular and enduring. But then, evangelical Christianity
changed: the Church became an institution that exercised the monopoly of power, using the name of God to wage wars, torture innocent
souls, and perform every type of atrocity.

The Lutheran Reform arose precisely to combat the excessive power
which had become cynical, hypocritical and arrogant. No more li-
tanies, no more contemplation of a longed-for paradise: those who
desired salvation had to earn it on this earth through concrete actions
and tangible virtue. Man should no longer look into his own soul, but
aspire to accumulating benefits for himself and the good of the community, in order to give glory to God.

Machiavelli placed morality aside in favour of power. This was the
birth of modern political science and its most important aspect: effi-
cacy. But if the end remains undetermined, power becomes an end in
itself. We should remember that even for Hobbes: "political power is
absolute and wields total power". And that is the perspective of the
sovereign whose action is the combination of creating and enforcing
power. But also for Hobbes, content had little importance: he who
rules has an exceptional status and cannot be called upon to answer for
his actions or intentions. Once again, as in religion, political power has
a tendency to generate a concentration of disasters.

After having ruled within religion and politics, the two forms of
power then moved on to the new religion: technology, assisted by
science and finance within the framework of globalization. We no
longer imagine what will appear when we finally reach the top of the
mountain; we remain focussed on the pegs we are hammering into the

rock face, one after another. "Growth", that mantra of the techno-logical era in which we live, is above all focused on size. Anything that is small or medium-sized is absorbed by something far bigger, among fusions and acquisitions that give life to landscapes composed only of skyscrapers. However, it also refers to fragmentation because "every-thing is destined to unravel, to be broken into pieces, into components: relationships, meanings, institutions". Lastly, it also refers to accel-eration, like skating on ice (an image invented by Bauman) and if we do not want to fall, we must proceed rapidly. The insurmountable problem is the fact that this all lacks any form of sense, and the per-fection that we relentlessly demand of ourselves through steel-willed self-discipline, to reach the standards which permit us to "be a part of the action" is inevitably destined to deteriorate because of our im-perfect, weak and mortal human nature.

Environmental sustainability: Bauman and Bandura

Speaking on environmental sustainability, Bauman was very clear in his endorsement of "Extractivism, Naomi Klein's apt term for the still dominant paradigm: a non reciprocal, dominance-based relationship with the earth, one purely of taking". If he had not died so suddenly, Bauman would have written the preface to *Moral Disengagement*,[15] the latest book by the greatest living social psychologist, Albert Bandura, who was the same age. These two giants drew their water from dif-ferent wells when one considers that Bandura is a cognitive psychol-ogist while Bauman was Freudian. However, they followed the same moral compass and often reached similar conclusions.

According to Bandura: "in conservative environmentalism, human ex-ceptionalism – human domination over nature – is the natural order. Nature is a resource that individuals and societies can own and use in pursuit of their self-interest. Markets place a value on nature".[16] This also applies for certain conservative Christians: "As one tea party supporter said, 'Being a strong Christian, I cannot help but believe the Lord placed a lot of minerals in our country and it's *[sic]* not there to destroy us'. [...] another adherent cited the Bible in arguing that global warming 'is a flat out lie'. He continued, 'I read my Bible. He made this earth for us to utilize'".[17]

It is not surprising, that like Bauman, Bandura quoted Pope Francis: "Pope Francis's encyclical *Laudato si'* (Praise be to you) calls climate change a worldwide problem. He condemns industrialized nations' heedless destruction of the environment purely for commer-cial gain and points out that the poor suffer the most from environ-mental degradation".[18]

What is certain is the fact that current generations are engaging in environmental degrading practices that will make life worse for future generations. "This foreshortened, self-centred perspective is captured in a jesting banner hung from a free-way bridge: 'What have future generations done for us?'".[19]

Where Bauman lashed out, drawing inspiration from dystopian narrative, Bandura took certain initiatives like those of Portera or educative narration by psychosocial means, to acquire new styles of behaviour and change pre-existing ones, in particular using long-running serial dramas. "These dramatic productions are not just fanciful stories. The plot lines portray the realities of people's everyday struggles, fears and aspirations, as well as the positive and negative effects of various social practices. [...] Hundreds of episodes spanning several years allow listeners and viewers to form strong emotional bonds with the cast-members models, whose thinking and behaviour evolve at a believable pace, inspiring and enabling viewers to improve their own lives".[20] Bandura began creating these serials with the help of directors and screenwriters like Sabido in Mexico, where in only two years, almost two million people learned to read and write thanks to literacy centres promoted by the main actors of the fiction series, after each episode was broadcast.

He then continued to produce serials and radio dramas (especially in Africa, where it is easier to listen to the radio than see TV programmes) teaching family planning, which necessarily touched the broader issue of the role and status of women.

"Characters in the dramas include models exhibiting beneficial, dysfunctional or transitional patterns of behavior. By dramatizing alternative behaviors and their effects on the characters' lives, the dramas help people make informed choices in their own lives. Viewers and listeners are especially likely to draw inspiration from, and identify with, transitional models who overcome adverse life circumstances like their own".[21]

I find the notion of using narrative to improve people's lives especially fascinating. Naturally, while I am extremely fond of Agostino Portera and Albert Bandura, and despite the admiration I have for their work, I tend to agree with the lessons of my *maestro* Bauman, who like Jonathan Franzen and Zadie Smith, considered that literature and narratives *cannot* change the world, or at least not alone. He felt that dystopias were more convincing in provoking self-questioning, uncertainty and unexpected shocks of awareness than plain and simple "educative" narrative. On this subject, I would like to quote a very powerful and appropriate example which I wrote about in my book with Tariq Ramadan *Il musulmano e l'agnostico.*[22] It is Bruno Arpaia's novel, *Qualcosa là fuori.*[23] Based on well-founded scientific fact, the author imagines that within 7 years, global warming will have submerged coastal areas, created deserts in temperate climates, made the whole of Africa *off limits,* and thanks to ice cap melting, Hyperborean zones will assume a pleasant Mediterranean climate. Consequently, those people who are refusing migrants and refugees today, will find themselves in the same migratory conditions, while Sweden, once the land of bloodthirsty warriors, today an example of civilization and welfare, will once again assume the characteristics of its past, and will re-introduce slavery. This is not science fiction but climate fiction, in other words, the prefiguration of plausible and even probable scenarios based on scientific facts available today. Arpaia's narrative is similar to the book by Michel Houellebecq: *The Possibility of an Island,* but describes the experiences of a young Italian scientist who travels to California, and witnesses the election of a president very similar to Donald Trump (although Arpaia wrote the book before Trump ran as candidate for the presidency). He finds himself expelled because of new Fascist anti-immigration laws, and experiences dramatic events following the disastrous climatic and geopolitical transformation of the planet.

Dystopias form a very powerful warning, and there is no doubt that if we are to take them into serious consideration, we must recover at least a part of our lost awareness.

Notes

1 Zygmunt Bauman and Riccardo Mazzeo, *On Education* (Cambridge: Polity Press, 2012).
2 Zygmunt Bauman and Riccardo Mazzeo, *In Praise of Literature* (Cambridge: Polity Press, 2016).
3 Zygmunt Bauman, *Liquid Modernity* (Cambridge: Polity Press, 2000, 2012).
4 Ibid., p. 206.
5 Ibid., p. 207.
6 Ibid., p. 208.
7 Zygmunt Bauman, *Strangers at Our Door* (Cambridge: Polity Press, 2016), p. 11.
8 Ibid., p. 32.
9 Zygmunt Bauman, *Intervista sull'identità (Interview on Identity),* ed. Benedetto Vecchi (Bari-Rome and Cambridge: Laterza and Polity Press, 2003), p. 13.
10 A. Portera, *Manuale di pedagogia interculturale* (Bari: Laterza, 2020); A. Portera, "Multicultural and Intercultural Education in Europe", in *Intercultural*

and Multicultural Education: Enhancing Global Interconnectedness, eds. C. A. Grant and A. Portera (New York: Routledge, 2011), pp. 12–32.

11 A. Portera, ed., *Competenze interculturali, Teoria e pratica nei settori scolastico-educativo, giuridico, aziendale, sanitario e della mediazione culturale* (Milan: FrancoAngeli, 2013); A. Portera, "Intercultural Competences in Education", in *Intercultural Education and Competences. Challenges and Answers for the Global World,* eds. A. Portera and C. A. Grant (Cambridge: Cambridge Scholars, 2017), pp. 8–26.

12 Debate in the book by Zygmunt Bauman and Agnes Heller, *La bellezza (non) ci salverà* (Trento: Il Margine, 2015).

13 Ibid., pp. 14–15.

14 Mauro Magatti, *Oltre l'infinito. Storia della potenza dal sacro alla tecnica* (Milan: Feltrinelli, 2018).

15 Albert Bandura, *Moral Disengagement: How People Do Harm and Live With Themselves* (New York: Worth Publishers, 2016).

16 Ibid., pp. 372–373.

17 Ibid., p. 374.

18 Ibid.

19 Ibid., p. 392.

20 Ibid., p. 416.

21 Ibid., p. 419.

22 Tariq Ramadan and Riccardo Mazzeo, *Il musulmano e l'agnostico* (Trento: Erickson, 2016).

23 Bruno Arpaia, *Qualcosa là fuori* (Parma: Guanda, 2016).

Part II

The dialogue between the authors

1 Risks and challenges of globalization, interdependence and cultural pluralism

Zygmunt Bauman and Agostino Portera

Agostino Portera: First of all, Professor Bauman, I would like to express my deep gratitude to you for having accepted my offer to co-author the present volume. The book is a result of a joint reflection on the greatest challenges of our times, of which you are one of the most expert and acute observers in the world. The purpose of the book is also to reflect together not only on the challenges and risks that exist but also on the possible answers. The book may be seen as an extension of our conversations that took place during the International Conference "Intercultural education and counselling in the global world",[1] where we had the opportunity to reflect on these changes and where you generously agreed to give the keynote speech.

Being as you are known as the discoverer of "liquid modernity", I believe that there can be no better start to our conversation than to reflect on the risks and opportunities of globalization and global interdependence. However, it is important to note that globalization also existed in the past; for instance one could think of the great empires of antiquity, such as the Roman Empire, which spread throughout the whole Mediterranean area and unified vast territories and cultures, or the opportunities for exchange, trade and human mobility after the so-called "discovery" of America, or the period of colonization during the 18th and 19th centuries. Today, the novel aspect is that, thanks to modern technology, we see a strong acceleration of the mobility – real and virtual – of goods, capital and people. The last decades have confirmed McLuhan's prophecy of 1962 regarding the advent of the "global village": the expansion of mass media, the accentuated potentiality of telecommunications, considerable shifts in geo-politics and nation states, and the emergence of new markets. These changes have led to a reduction in distances, a strengthening of the ties between different regions (acceleration, interdependence, unpredictability), greater mobility, an expansion and diversification of migratory flows, which permit new opportunities for the encounter (and sometimes, sadly, the clash) between the plurality of normative models, styles of interpersonal relations, lifestyles and completely foreign value systems.

Regarding these changes, it is necessary to underline that the growing pluralism in economy, science and religion involves not only serious risks, but also *opportunities* in respect of politics (different ways of life and widespread democratic government), healthcare (eradication of many diseases once considered incurable; increased life expectancy; lower infant mortality rates), economy (more prosperity and wealth in many countries of the world) and culture (growth of multiethnic and multicultural societies; more opportunities to travel, learn, explore, compare).

On the other hand, as you have rightfully stressed in numerous writings and public speeches, in addition to the above-mentioned advantages, our times are also accompanied by a set of problematic aspects. Regarding the economic and commercial profile of the third millennium, the protagonists of globalization are the industrial, military and space-age superpowers which compete for markets and profits at the expense of the most vulnerable. Multinational companies and the largest economies, by spreading their products to all corners of the earth, have disastrous effects on the fragile economic and social fabric of developing countries: increasing the poverty of many in order to generate wealth for a few, even within the same nation-state. Especially in Western societies, the dissolution of an "open" and democratic society is becoming increasingly evident. While within the context of K. Popper's 1944 book, *The Open Society and Its Enemies,* this crisis evolved from the threat of authoritarian regimes like Nazi Germany and the Soviet Union, now the greatest threat seems to come from the "fundamentalism of the market". G. Soros[2] denounces the prevalence of profit seeking and a decline of collective decision-making according to a principle of "reflexivity": rather than just passively reflecting reality, markets construct the reality that they reflect. Given the presence of a global economy in the absence of a "global society", incursions of the market economy in various areas of civil society arise, causing "destructive and demoralizing" effects.[3] New technologies lead to a less serene management of human resources: robots replace workers; machines replace controllers; distance learning and computers replace teachers. In a short time the work of a subject (a basic element of its identity) appears to be distorted. The sense of connection to a company, to a political party, to a country (who can now still speak of a homeland?), even to a spouse or to a family is severely weakened. The state of insecurity and impermanence, the knowledge that everything can be commodified and monetized, is detrimental to the satisfaction of basic human needs (especially the need for a sense of belonging[4]). The professional insecurity (fear of mobility or being fired) often leads to work overload (more time, stress, anxiety, irritability).

Among the many challenges in the globalized world, one of the most difficult ones, which I would like to start thinking about with you, is the need to face "cultural diversity". Due to the advent of some changes, as the Internet and low-cost flights, it is no longer necessary to travel the old way; the "stranger", the "different" are in our home, in our condominium, in our city. For understanding the phenomena of encounter and clash better, it is appropriate to pause and reflect upon the most evident cultural changes of our late-modern time.

In order to look more specifically at the cultural level, it is necessary to start off with the basic premise that all societies of the world today should be recognized as multiethnic and multicultural. We should begin from the fact that in the world in which we are living homogeneous cultures or different races have never existed. Although the concept of "race" is still erroneously used in many parts of the word — especially in the Anglophone (most of all in the North American) context — in reality different races do not exist, and humans certainly cannot be categorized hierarchically. The most plausible description of the history of human beings assumes a permanent network of exchanges, not only cultural, but also genetic, between different populations. According to the most reliable studies of palaeontology, archaeology, historical linguistics and genetics,[5,6] the common origin of *all* women and men would be in the area between Southern Africa, East Africa and the Near East. Therefore, especially in humanities, the most dangerous misconception (and scientific error) regarding the existence of several races (often classified according to skin colour and facial features) must be definitively deconstructed: *the only race on earth is the human race.*

Nevertheless, if it is true that human beings are *tous parents*, then it is also true that we are *tous différents*[7]: over the millennia significant changes at a somatic and especially at a cultural level have occurred, as a result of geography, food sources, social organization, etc. Furthermore the concepts of culture and identity are not static, as they change over time. For example, by closely observing Western societies, the ongoing changes in the "liquid-modern" world, which you have rightfully talked about in many of your works, turn out to be so destabilizing that they could be compared to the Industrial Revolution of the 19th century, both in terms of scope and intensity. Digital technology has changed all aspects of human life, and biotechnology is going to change life itself. Global trade, travel and communication opportunities are deeply modifying the cultural horizons of all people and social groups of the countries involved. With the advent of multiethnic and multicultural societies and the fulfilment of the idea of a "global village", human beings can nowadays choose between very different lifestyles, or share their ideas with men and women who live thousands of miles away from them, sometimes people they have never met.

Meanwhile, in the most industrialized Western societies, a change in terms of rules, values and modes of interaction is taking place: life seems to be more and more accompanied by feelings of insecurity and uncertainty; stable relationships and the ability to manage stress and frustration are decreasing; financial, economic, political and environmental crises as well as crises linked to culture, identity and the meaning of human existence are increasing in frequency and effect. The cause and consequence of these crises, which is often a cultural and identity crisis, is the medicalization of life that aims to solve any kind of problems. When diseases and illnesses, as well as simple malaise, conflicts or difficulties (including learning difficulties in school) started occurring, pharmaceutical companies immediately began providing quick and "painless" solutions. It seems that all problems involve molecular diseases and need to be tackled by paying a large sum of money and by hiring more and more specialists; everything seems to aim at profit, at economic gain.

In your analysis of these cultural changes, for example, in *Society Under Siege*[8] and *Liquid Love,*[9] you clearly explain how globalization and technical and cultural dominance lead to a "liquid modernity", resulting in flexible identities that are able to quickly adapt to every situation, and in "liquid loves" that are incapable of perseverance, commitment and making plans. The constant desire to change and the need to do it immediately are harmful to long-standing relationships. There are no elements of planning, building and preservation of a given order. There are no value systems with which everyone can identify. The new global elite floats, naturally moves to many countries in the world, quickly surfs the Internet. Its members are not tied to the sense of territory: their reference points are moving and fleeting, both physically and spiritually; their loyalty to people, places and nation-states is also fleeting. In cyberspace there are no topoi, no borders and no border posts. Membership of the global elite is defined by their disengagement and their freedom from binding commitments. The highest values of modernity, such as fixedness, duration, solidity and stability have all been rejected and have taken on a negative connotation.

These considerations have been further elaborated upon during your highly esteemed speech at the conference in Verona,[10] where you presented a not-so-rosy view of the future, as the certainties our fathers had cannot be taken for granted anymore. Quoting Stephen Bertman[11] you use the terms "nowist culture" and "hurried culture". In our liquid-modern society human beings, more than in any other historical period, have the unique opportunity to *re-negotiate the meaning of time*. For the current "consumer society", time is neither linear nor circular, as it was perceived throughout history up to pre-modern and modern societies, but *pointillist*. Nowadays time is broken up into a multitude of pieces, each piece reduced to a single point closely approximating its geometric ideal of non-dimensionality, lacking in length, size or depth. Meanwhile every single point seems to expand as a "big bang", full of opportunities, regardless of what happened in the previous point. As you rightly state, in this scenario, "the rates of infant mortality and miscarriages of hopes are very high". Each point is lived as a new beginning, an unrestrained expansion of new beginnings. This change also involves the moment of being "born again"; in this way the past and the previous lives can be erased: "What one was yesterday, would no longer bear the possibility of becoming someone totally different today". We are therefore witnessing the beginning of the current late-modern tyranny of *carpe diem*, which is replacing the pre-modern tyranny of *memento mori*.

Given this situation, apart from your reaction and feedback on my comments above, I would like to reflect with you on two aspects. First of all, I am wondering if we might be risking being partial and unilateral in analyzing the alarming negative effects of globalization and of global interdependence. Perhaps we are too pessimistic, possibly influenced by the mass media, which only highlight the distressing aspects of policy, economy and news (crises and catastrophes in order to fuel fears that foster consumption and underpin the market, in order to get more viewers or sell more newspapers). Maybe we are not spending enough time highlighting the positive aspects, the beauty, the joy of existing, the great fortune (for many people on earth at least) and the great opportunity of living in a time of peace, democracy (achieved through the sacrifice, even the death of millions of our relatives, parents and grandparents), and cultural pluralism, while analyzing the present time. The second consideration involves the hope that we can give in the analysis of the present times. Can you give your personal opinion on what we all, everyone with their own role and responsibilities, as inhabitants of this world (the only planet we know so far where life exists), can and must do so that opportunities for all individuals and the human species may arise from the many current challenges and crises (economic, political, environmental, cultural, identity crisis), and from life in pluralistic and multicultural societies?

Zygmunt Bauman: You call us to remember that the current liquid-modern mode of the human condition contains "not only serious risks, but also *opportunities*". I'd add: just like the human condition in all its past, and in all probability all its future avatars. Risks and opportunities are inseparable twins – when you spot one of them, look around and you can be sure of finding the other, salient or hidden, running the show or hiding in the wings. As the English say, you can't eat a cake and have it; or as all tribal wisdoms warn, you can't get something for nothing: for every gain, its costs. Simultaneously with inventing railways, we invented train catastrophes; with cars – road crashes; with airplanes – the air disasters. Recently, my wife's electric riser/recliner chair went bust; I learned on this occasion that the introduction of such chairs gave birth to a new category of engineers – a new profession requiring novel and quite complex skills; so even the technologically advanced chairs had both positive and negative consequences all of their own: new objects at risk of going wrong, and an opportunity for a new expertise and employment chances. All in all, each successive departure, big or small, in the modality of human-being-in-the world entails risks and opportunities of its own kind.

It might be said that what you in fact entreat us to do is to play, intermittently, the two distinct roles of the two kinds of record-keepers – distinguished by the ancient sages under the names of eu-colons and dis-colons. A colon signals adding the evaluating to the merely descriptive intention. It means "that is to say" or "here's what I mean" – as Jane Straus, the author of the highly esteemed, indeed standard-setting *The Blue Book of Grammar and Punctuation* instructs us. Sitting down in the evening to record the events of the day, which they both spent from dawn to dusk in each other's company, exposed to exactly the same experiences, a "eucolon" would include in the list primarily the occurrences he/she considers good and well, while a "discolon" would focus on what he/she found disparaging and off-putting.

I admit to lean to the "discolon" side. This could be a matter of personal character, or perhaps of my early encounter with, and since then a continuing attachment to critical philosophy and sociology. But it might be as well (as I would like it to be) the result of a meditation on the springs of social/historical change, particularly of the "change to the better". Barrington Moore Jr.[12] pointed out that in the opposition between justice and injustice it is the second term that is "unmarked": holds priority. Our ideas − visions, ideal models − of "justice", and the postulates they inspire, are prompted and shaped at every stage of history and in every part of society by the experience of such states of affairs, conditions or events, which people find unprepossessing, disgraceful, abominable, repulsive and outraging: in short, unjust. It is the expanding intolerance to injustice that results in the expansion of justice. The snag is that recognition of things as unjust and of injustice as avoidable does not come out of itself and is not easy to attain when tried. For philosophers whom we retrospectively acknowledge to have been the founders of humanities, as well as for statesmen of the 18th-Century America whom we praise as the founders of modern democracy, rebellion against slavery was a violation of divine and/or natural order and a severely punishable crime. For the most enlightened and high-minded political leaders of the European 19th and early 20th century, keeping women out of the political body and out of public life was again a verdict of nature, whereas dissent against it was a noxious crime, as the British suffragettes learned the hard way. And so to enlist people to the cause of justice, you need first to open their eyes to the injustices of the status quo; you need to prompt them to re-classify things seemed to be "natural", "unavoidable" and "immutable" and all too often deemed to be "right and proper", as unjust and utterly avertable and escapable. This is, arguably, the toughest part of the task. And as William Pitt the Younger put it when addressing the House of Commons on 18 November 1783, "necessity [inevitability and irrevocability] is the plea for every infringement of human freedom. It is the argument of tyrants; it is the creed of slaves". All in all, I believe that being on the "discolon" side is to be wholeheartedly recommended. After all, the road to the better starts at the point of refusal to condone and endure the worse. Any attempt of finding/inventing an answer to your most exigent and eminently poignant question "what we all, everyone with their own role and responsibilities [...] can and must do so that opportunities for all individuals and the human race may arise from the many current challenges and crises [...] and from life in pluralistic and multicultural must begin from there".

You flawlessly pinpoint many of the most harrowing aspects of the present-day condition as both avoidable and overdue for a thorough overhaul. Among them, "the presence of a global economy in the absence of a global society", and the "severely weakened" "sense of connection" − particularly the secession of "the new global elite" from their heretofore local households into a formless and to a great extent lawless no-man's land of the Manuel Castells' "space of flows". In the effect, it is as if Goethe's wide-eyed yet artless and ignorant

Zauberlehrling (sorcerer's apprentice) during a protracted absence of the Master, sets the brooms in motion yet fails to stop them, causing flood and general havoc all around: once set in motion by humans, technology develops its own momentum, disposing of its designers and producers: "New technologies", as you correctly point out, "lead to a less serene management of human resources: robots replace workers; machines replace controllers; distance learning and computers replace teachers". And under selectively globalized conditions (globalization of power but not politics) there is no "master" in sight capable of checking – let alone to deter – their antics. Unless politics (the capacity of selecting things for being done) is raised to the scale of powers (capacities of having things done), already globalized and therefore left out of political control, there is little chance for the master returning from his overlong leave.

In the meantime – as long as the incongruence of global economy combined with locally confined politics, or economic interdependence coinciding with the phantom of local independence, persists – there is little (some say next to none) defence measures which people already suffering the effects or under the threat of being next in the line to suffer them can reasonably expect from the political institutions which our ancestors developed for serving the territorially sovereign nation-states. For all practical intents and purposes, the "really existing" globalization would better be described as a process of glocalization: denuding localities of their power goes hand in hand with over-burdening local politics with tasks they lack the resources to tackle. Today's problems are generated globally, but it is left to local authorities to cope with their effects, or at least try to do so. Whatever happens, they would bear in any case an undivided responsibility for eventual failure.

One of numerous globally generated problems with which the slim and frail local capacities are confronted are the socio-cultural consequences of – as you put it – "the 'stranger', the 'different' [arriving and settling] in our home, in our condominium, in our city". A star example, by the way, of your risk and opportunity rolled into one. Migrants incoming to the densely populated (and more often than not big) cities (for the first time in history, the majority of humans reside in such urban places) are neither willing nor pushed or ordered to "assimilate", that is to renounce their identities and particular/peculiar lifestyles, but retain their differences. Contemporary migration sediments "diasporization" of the planet. Close daily proximity of different ethnicities, religions, languages, collective memories and historically formed modes of life create an ambiance of anxiety and mutual suspicion. "Stranger", by definition, is an entity insufficiently familiar and for that reason carrier of uncertainty and so vague, undefined, difficult to pinpoint threat: stranger is a priori a suspicious being, guilty until proved (or rather proving himself) innocent. The psychological effect is "mixophobia" − horror of mixing and urge for territorial separation, which as a rule acquires a self-reinforcing momentum of its own: the less the members of different diasporised communities associate and communicate with each other, the less skills of conversing, ability of understanding and will to meet, associate and team up they possess; a state of mind and emotions which in turn beefs up the mutual mistrust and fear and prompts them to expand and deepen. The opportunity of "mixophilia" − of face-to-face, point-blank, earnest and sincere encounter leading to a meaningful dialogue and mutual comprehension, fusion of horizons and reciprocal spiritual enrichment − faces thereby the danger of being wasted. A danger − though under no condition a necessity. Mixing with difference has its multiple attractions and holds quite a few tempting promises. Mixophilic tendencies, prodded by sharing the streets, workplaces, schools, and public spaces of the city are never stifled completely − they may only go underground in times of occasional, similarly unpreventable infractions of mutual mistrust and grievance. The impacts of the two psychological responses to the same condition of urban life are finely balanced; it is virtually impossible to presage which of the two is set to prevail and for how long. We do face risks and opportunities in one indivisible package deal. Here you are − take it or leave it.

We do live currently in a probably irrevocably and irreversibly multicultural world – a product of massive migration of ideas, values and beliefs, as well as their human carriers. Physical separation, if still conceivable (a moot question), no longer assures spiritual distance. "Their God" and "ours" have their respective temples built in each other's immediate neighbourhood – though inside the online universe in which we all spend an already considerable and still fast-swelling chunk of our waking time, all temples are located at the same distance, or more to the point in the same space-time proximity. We should be careful, however, to set apart the two notions all-too-often misleadingly deployed in public vocabulary interchangeably: multiculturality and multiculturalism. The first denotes realities (of surroundings, life-scene, ambiance); the second, an attitude, policy or life-strategy of choice. In his most recent oeuvre, one of the strongest Polish philosophers, Piotr Nowak,[13] subjects to a thorough vivisection Stanley Fish's the enfant terrible of the sedate establishment of scholarship, critique of the second of the pair: multiculturalist attitude and/or programme.[14]

Fish distinguishes two varieties of multiculturalism: "boutique" and "strong". The first is marked by the jarring contradiction between "politically correct" incantation of principles – which (in Nowak's words) "emphasize the importance of proper relations between coexisting cultures as well as the respect and sympathy allegedly bestowed upon them; on the other hand, however, throttles rage and allergy aroused by the genuine disparities found vexing and offending". And, dedicated as it insists to be to principles of tolerance, neutrality, impartiality, open-mindedness and fairness and convinced (wrongly) of their universality, "boutique multiculturalism" fails to comprehend others who treat their – however idiosyncratic and repellent – convictions and life routines seriously and cling to them really devotedly, rigidly and tightly. The second, strong version of multiculturalism goes, so to speak, the whole hog: it accords every culture an infrangible and indisputable right to practice whatever it considers right and proper, as well as barring all external critique, let alone interference, of the practices this or that culture promotes. As Nowak comments, a "strong" multiculturalist falls into a trap from which for her or him there is no escape: would he/she go as far as allowing the cannibals to eat the meat they like most? But let us give voice to Fish himself in *The Trouble with Principle*:

> Boutique multiculturalism is the multiculturalism of ethnic restaurants, weekend festivals, and high-profile flirtations with the other in the manner satirized by Tom Wolfe under the rubric "radical chic". Boutique multiculturalism is characterized by its superficial or cosmetic relationship to the objects of its affection. Boutique multiculturalists admire or appreciate or enjoy or sympathize with or (at the very least) "recognize the legitimacy of" the traditions of cultures other than their own; but boutique multiculturalists will always stop short of approving other cultures at a point where some value at their center generates an act that offends against the canons of civilized decency as they have been either declared or assumed.[15]

> The politics of difference [a term coined by Charles Taylor] is what I mean by strong multiculturalism. It is strong because it values difference in and for itself [...] Whereas the boutique multiculturalist will accord a superficial to cultures other than his own – a respect that he will withdraw when he finds the practices of a culture irrational or inhumane – a strong multiculturalist will want to accord a *deep* respect to all cultures at their core, for he believes that each has the right to form its own identity and nourish its own sense

of what is rational and humane. For the strong multiculturalist, the first principle is not rationality [...] but tolerance.[16]

As Nowak sums this up, "either a boutique multiculturalism, or none, as the strong multiculturalism is impossible – though its boutique alternative is but a pretence". To conclude: multiculturality is reality, and a tough one, that can hardly be chased away or wished away. Differentiation of values and of the criteria of setting apart the proper from the improper, humane from inhumane and the decent from the indecent, as well as the awesome holding power of firm convictions and communal solidarities are indeed facts of life. But "multiculturalism" in its dual manifestation of a standpoint and a policy, both calculated to inform and trigger practices able to detoxify the unprepossessing consequences of that reality set a site for a tension- and anxiety-ridden minefield rather than a (multi)theme amusement park. Coming to terms with the migration, which in the absence of a viable policy (and indeed willingness) of assimilation cannot but result in the progressive diasporization of the life-scene, a skeleton key opening all doors or a panacea curing all the inner contradictions and cognitive dissonances such life-scene is capable (and prone) of generating, is highly unlikely to be found. The art of peaceful, antagonisms-free and mutually gratifying cohabitation is short on the once-for-all valid rules and long on uncertainties, risks and frictions as well as the needs of improvisation. It also takes time – considerable time – to devise and learn such art, with little hope for ever reaching the conclusion of the designing and learning effort that would render further swatting and sweating redundant.

But to come back to the question you addressed to me: am I exceedingly, or too one-sidedly, pessimistic?

Jorge Luis Borges, one of the greatest writers ever and in my mind the greatest philosopher among storytellers, inimitable in his talent of spotting the universe in a grain of sand, wrote among hundreds of little masterpieces also a short story called "The Lottery in Babylon".[17] I am sure you know that short story (of the anonymous narrator? of human predicament?), but for the benefit of our possible readers, let me recall its essential ideas.

"I have known", the narrator declares, "that things that Greeks knew not – uncertainty". Why did they know not? Because they invented the way of squeezing the poison out of the sting of that pest, uncertainty. "Heraclides Ponticus reports, admiringly, that Pythagoras recalled having been Pyrrhus, and before that, Euphorbus, and before that, some other mortal; in order to recall similar vicissitudes, I have no need of death, nor even of imposture. I owe that almost monstrous

variety to an institution – the Lottery". Lottery, we are given to surmise, is an institution that recycles mortal life in an unending string of
new beginnings. Each new beginning portends new risks, but in a
package deal with new opportunities. None of the beginnings is ulti-
mate and irrevocable: there is always another one blinking round the
corner. Thanks to the Lottery, many lives can be accommodated in the
life of a single mortal. The awesome, harrowing spectre of uncertainty
is thereby chased away; or rather re-moulded from a most horrifying
liability into a rapturous, elating asset.

Lottery is the gambling incarnate. Instead of more of the same, you
opt, by buying a ticket, for the new; and you sign a blank cheque, not
for you to fill it up. It has, as the narrator admits, "no moral force
whatsoever". It "appealed not to all a man's faculties, but only to his
hopefulness". The owners of lottery tickets "might win a sum of
money or they might be required to pay a fine". No wonder, there was
quite a few gutless, mean-spirited Babylonians who preferred to settle
for what they already had and to desist the temptation of more wealth –
and so steered clear of Lottery offices. Men who run the Lottery
resorted, however, to a blackmail of sorts: they managed to cause a
man who bought none of the Lottery tickets to be widely censured as
"a pusillanimous wretch, a man with no spirit of adventure". Though
they didn't stop at such half-measure. "Lottery was made secret, free
of charge, and open to all"; most importantly, "every free man auto-
matically took part in the sacred drawings". From then on, The
Company (running the Lottery) "with godlike modesty shuns all
publicity. Its agents, of course, are secret; the orders it constantly
(perhaps continually) imparts are no different from those spread
wholesale by impostors". For all the Babylonians know, or imagine, or
surmise, or suspect – "the Lottery is an interpolation of chance into
the order of the universe". And so it goes for them without saying that
"to accept errors is to strengthen chance, not contravene it". True,
some "masked heresiarchs" heretics go on whispering that "*the
Company has never existed, and never will*"; other heretics, though –
"no less despicable" – argue that "it makes no difference whether one
admits or denies the reality of the shadowy corporation, because
Babylon is nothing but an infinite game of chance".

Well, I feel inclined to sign up to those "other heretics'" club. It seems
that we are all Babylonians now, whether by design or by default, and
for reasons which you yourself rightly spotted: we are "gamblers" by
decree of fate (or, more correctly, by our – and our modern ancestors –
past choices ossified into human condition). And we owe it to most
clearheaded minds among us, of Borges' calibre, to be reminded that this

is the case. And lottery, as I guess and hope you'd agree, is the very epitome of mixing risks with opportunities and making them fully and truly inseparable.

Notes

1 The International Congress "Intercultural education and counselling in the global world" was held in Verona from 15 to 18 April 2013 and organized by the Centre for Intercultural Studies, University of Verona (www. csiunivr.eu), in cooperation with OISE-Ontario Institute for Studies in Education: University of Toronto, the International Association for Intercultural Education (IAIE) and the National-American Association for Multicultural Education (NAME). It was attended by around 160 speakers (including some of the top experts in the field) and 400 members from all continents and most countries of the world (Italy, England, Holland, Germany, Spain, Portugal, Sweden, Denmark, Switzerland, Malta, Greece, Canada, USA, Russia, Africa, India, South America, Israel, Sri Lanka, UAE, Bahrain, Estonia, etc.).

2 G. Soros, *The Crisis of Global Capitalism* (New York: Perseus Books, 1998) pp. 20, 33–39.

3 Ibid., pp. 33–95.

4 In a longitudinal qualitative research on the acquisition of identity in multi-cultural context, carried out in Germany with young people of Italian origin, has emerged the importance of the satisfaction of certain needs, including especially the need of belonging, in order to take benefit from the situation that has changed. A. Portera, *Tesori sommersi. Emigrazione, identità, bisogni educativi interculturali* 4th ed. (Milan: FrancoAngeli, 2005) (1st ed., 1997), p. 174; A. Portera, *Interkulturelle Identitäten. Empirische Untersuchung über Risiko- und Schutzfaktoren der Identitätsbildung italienischer Jugendlicher in Südbaden und in Süditalien* (Köln: Böhlau-Verlag, 1995).

5 R. Lewontin, *La diversité génétique humaine* (Berlin: Puf, 1984).

6 L. e F. Cavalli Sforza, *Chi siamo. La storia della diversità umana* (Milano: Mondadori, 1993).

7 *Tous parents – tous différents* was the Motto of an exhibition by the Musée National d'histoire naturelle – Musée de l'homme, Paris, from March 1992 to August 1995.

8 Z. Bauman, *Society Under Siege* (Cambridge: Polity Press, 2002).

9 Z. Bauman, *Liquid Love: On the Frailty of Human Bonds* (Cambridge: Polity Press, 2003).

10 Z. Bauman, "Liquid Modern Challenges to Education", in *Intercultural Education and Competences: Challenges and Answers for the Global World*, eds. A. Portera and C. A. Grant (Newcastle: Cambridge Scholars, 2016).

11 S. Bertman, *Hyperculture: The Human Cost of Speed* (Westport: Praeger, 1998).

12 See Barrington Moore Jr., *Injustice: The Social Bases of Obedience and Revolt* (New York: M. E. Sharpe, 1978).

13 Piotr Nowak, *Hodowanie troglodytów* (*Breeding Troglodytes*) (Warsaw: Fundacja Augusta Hrabiego Cieszkowskiego, 2014).

14 See Stanley Fish, "Boutique Multiculturalism, or Why Liberals Are

Incapable of Thinking about Hate Speech", *Critical Inquiry* 23, no. 2 (Winter 1997), pp. 378–395; Stanley Fish, *The Problem with Principle* (Cambridge: Harvard UP, 1999).

15 Stanley Fish, *The Problem with Principle* (Cambridge: Harvard UP, 1999), p. 56.

16 Ibid., p. 60.

17 Quoted by me in Andrew Hurley's translation – see *Collected Fictions* (London: Allen Lane, 1999), pp. 101–106.

2 Religious pluralism

Clash of civilizations or opportunity of encounter? Relational, not hierarchical approach

Zygmunt Bauman and Agostino Portera

Agostino Portera: Although our common reflection does not only deal with risks and problems but also focuses on the positive aspects and opportunities, I totally agree with you, dear Prof. Bauman: "to enlist people to the cause of justice, you need first to open their eyes to the injustices of the status quo; you need to prompt them to re-classify things seemed to be 'natural', 'unavoidable' and 'immutable' and all too often deemed to be 'right and proper', as unjust and utterly avertable and escapable". Raising awareness among the causes of injustice and "wishing up to the reality" are necessary to revaluate aspects that seem natural, inviolable or immutable, making them completely avoidable and unnecessary. In fact, knowing the dynamic of the issues not only makes people more pessimistic, but – on the contrary – can also represent the beginning of an awareness that allows one to better reflect on the strategies needed to find a solution. Therefore, it could be appropriate to dedicate part of the present book to a better explanation and analysis of some of the "evils" of our times, and of the liquid-modern society which you have described several times. Another part could then contain a further reflection on the possible solutions.

By following the news, I think an extremely topical issue is the relationship between different religions. The beginning of 2015 has been characterized by tragic (apparently) religiously-motivated events. On the 8th of January two men armed with Kalashnikov assault rifles entered the offices of the satirical weekly magazine *Charlie Hebdo* in Paris, shouting "Allah u akbar" (God is great), and randomly shot at those in the office, killing 12 people and injuring about ten, half of them seriously. The perpetrators, masked and clad in black, spoke fluent French. In the massacre four newspaper cartoonists died: the director Stephan Charbonnier (nicknamed Charb), Jean Cabut (Cabu), Tignous and Georges Wolinski. Coming out of the offices, the two men killed two policemen and drove off in a car. The supposed "crime" of the newspaper and the journalists was that they had published cartoons on religious issues, including a cartoon depicting the prophet Mohammed.

The following day, Amedy Coulibaly, another fundamentalist who was associated with the *Charlie Hebdo* attackers, barricaded himself with hostages in a Jewish Kosher supermarket in Vincennes, a small city outside Paris. In addition to the attacker, who was killed by police, four hostages died. In a video posted on the Web, the perpetrator of the massacre claimed he was a member of Isis and aimed to commit a massacre in a Jewish kindergarten. ISIS is an acronym that stands for the Islamic State of Iraq and al-Sham, also known as the Islamic State of Iraq and Syria, or the Islamic State of Iraq and Levant (ISIL). It is a jihadist group (soldiers of the "holy war") operating in Syria and Iraq which uses violence and terror to meet their goals. The current leader, Abu Bakr al-Baghdadi, unilaterally announced the rebirth of the caliphate in the territories under his control. The United Nations and several nations have labelled Isis as a terrorist organization.

At the beginning of 2015, on the 10th of January, a ten-year-old girl strapped with explosives blew herself up and killed 20 people and injured about 50 in a market in Maiduguri, the capital of the Nigerian state of Borno. The following day the terrorists targeted a mobile phone market in the city of Potiskum, in the northeast state of Yobe, where two girls of about ten years of age blew themselves up in the crowd. In total three died and about 40 were wounded. The first noted case of a girl suicide bomber was on the 10th of December 2014, when a 13-year-old refused to blow herself up in a market in Kano and later said she had been "recruited" by her father to serve the "caliphate" of Boko Haram. *Boko Haram*, which in the Hausa language means "Western education is a sin", is a jihadist terrorist organization spread throughout the north of Nigeria, also known as the "Group of the Sunni People" for religious propaganda and Jihad. This is also in the name of the "Caliphate" that a group of Islamic terrorists wants to impose, through systematic "ethnic-religious cleansing". In the name of this terroristic organization, Islamic fundamentalist militiamen have also attacked Damaturu, the capital of the neighbouring state of Yobe, over the last months. About five weeks before the presidential and legislative elections in Nigeria, a group of jihadists terrorized the cities and the inhabitants of the northeast of the country, forcing thousands of people to migrate to the borders of Cameroon, Chad and Niger. In some villages of the region of Baga, in the far northeast of Nigeria, on the banks of Lake Chad, for example, a group of Boko Haram terrorists shot at everyone they saw for four days, leaving several thousand dead lying on the ground to "punish" the local militias who attempt to defend themselves.

In the following years, Isis and Boko Haram, "the 'world's most horrific terrorist group",[1] have been increasing the cooperation and terroristic acts, by sharing "machine guns, tactics, techniques and procedures" in order to conduct complex ambushes, set explosive devices, launch attacks on hotels and wage a bloody insurgency across parts of Africa. Statistics from Unicef show that the number of abused kamikaze children is getting higher every year, and research from BBC shows that Boko Haram provoked in 2017 over 150 attacks (127 attacks in 2016), most of all in Nigeria (109) and Cameroon.[2]

In his book *The Clash of Civilizations and the Remaking of World Order,* published in 1996, S. P. Huntington, professor at Harvard University and chairman of the Harvard Academy for International and Area Studies, states that in the new millennium we need a new model which is able to provide satisfactory explanations to the events that are taking place, as the previous models are no longer able to do so. He thinks[3] there are essentially four dominant models in the post-Cold war era: *just one world: euphoria and harmony,* according to which the end of the Cold war means the end of the major international conflicts and the birth of a harmonious world (a model stressed by F. Fukuyama in his theory on the end of world history); *two worlds: we and the others,* according to which human beings always tend to split reality into "us and them", the equal and the different, East and West, your own civilization and other people's cruelty; *184 Countries,* according to which the individual states are the key players, and each of them tries to extend its power; and *total chaos*, the individual states are constantly being weakened, and they will construct a world dominated by anarchy. Huntington thinks the four models are incompatible, full of limitations and shortcomings. He proposes considering the dominated world starting from the exiting civilizations that are: (a) Sinic civilization, which is of Chinese origin and dates back to 1500 B.C.; (b) Japanese civilization, which emerged between 100 and 400 A.C.; (c) Hindu civilization, which has been in India since 1500 B.C.; (d) Islamic civilization, which originated on the Arabian Peninsula in the 7th century A.C. and has spread to North Africa, the Iberian Peninsula, central Asia, India and Southeast Asia; (e) Western civilization, which dates back to 700 A.C. and has divided into European, North American and Latin-American civilizations; Latin-American civilization, which developed out of Western civilization, and is more corporate and authoritarian and rooted in Catholism, and which includes indigenous cultures; (f) African civilization, which is recognized by few researchers, but has spread to most of the African states, and has been characterized by the effects of religious missions, imperialism and colonization. The author believes[4] these cultural differences are strictly connected with the religious specificities that have recently returned to the fore as a reaction to laicism and moral relativism, proposing values such as order, discipline, mutual aid and solidarity. Huntington thinks that even religious fundamentalism, especially Islamic, represents a way to overcome the disorientation and the loss of identity caused by a rapid introduction of Western political and social models (laicism, scientism, economic development). As a result, he identifies the clash of civilizations as the central challenge of the present and the future, defining it as a "serious threat to the world peace"[5] in the post-Cold War world. As the management of differences – among which the religious difference is considered of primary importance – between these seven or eight civilizations represents the main challenge, he also urges the major civilizations of the world, especially Europe and United States, to stand together.

I think Huntington's reflections help to understand part of the problem but also present some risks. First of all, there seems to be a hazard of human beings being classified according to nationality, thus pointing out our differences or possibly even hierarchically organized civilizations (and once again we come back to the insidious concept of "race"). As it has already been said, cultures are neither homogeneous, nor static, nor confined to continents or nation-states. Human history is based on migration, and the history of civilization has always been characterized by cross-cultural exchange and fertilization (although not always peaceful). Defining the concepts of "good" and "evil" would be just as dangerous nowadays. Fundamentalism does not only exist in the Islamic context. As nowadays, fortunately, many (also religious) sources rightfully stress, an association between Islam and these terroristic acts would be very foolhardy. By reflecting on these events, I think cultural differences, including religious differences, are often used as an alibi to justify acts of violence whose real causes should be sought elsewhere. In the period of brutal terrorist attacks connected with fascism or communism, which involved many European countries in the 1960s and 1970s (Red Brigades or New Order in Italy), no one ever associated these groups of people to a nation-state, a religion, or a political party. Stamping out terrorism was made possible because the majority of citizens, even those with similar political or cultural affiliation, differentiated themselves from the terrorists. Nowadays, even many influential commentators seem to be falling into the trap of simplifying what is in fact a complex process. That is, they disregard the reality that individual human beings or small groups can carry out such brutal criminal acts of violence for several reasons, rather than religious or cultural: mental disorders, fanaticism, power struggles, economic interests, conditioning, manipulation, etc.

Nevertheless, dear Zygmunt, I think a reflection with you on the religious issue would be useful, as it currently represents one of the main challenges of our times. If by religion we mean the set of beliefs that constitute an expression of faith and absolute acceptance of the truth, the believer, but also the layman or the atheist, cannot avoid thinking that all other people's faiths or non-faiths are wrong. Conflict, therefore, seems inevitable.[6]

The history of the Catholic Church, for example, has been characterized by violent phenomena for ages. Just think of the periods of Crusades, defined as "holy wars" against non-believers, the Inquisition when brutal torture was used, or the Witch Hunts when women denounced as witches were burned at the stake. After the last World War, the Protestant Christian churches proposed a meeting with the advocate of the other Christian religions (in Amsterdam, 1948). The outcome was quite negative, because of the disagreement between the faiths taking part, as well because of the official absence of the Catholic Church. A decisive change in the attitude of the Catholic Church towards the other traditions of Christianity did not happen until after the Second Vatican Ecumenical Council in the Sixties, when, at the suggestion of Pope John XXIII, the church decided to shift its attitude and started to stress the common elements of Christianity rather than the differences. Emphasis was placed on the importance of mutual knowledge as a chance for understanding, overcoming disagreements, and for cooperation based upon fundamental and shared values. Since the Second Vatican Council, Christian unity,[7] common beliefs among Christians and Jews,[8] understanding between Christians and Muslims,[9] as well as cooperation between believers and non-believers[10] have been fostered. These policies have been furthered by subsequent Popes, among whom Pope Francis is a great example of openness and willingness. The developments relating to the fostering of interreligious encounter and dialogue also concern nowadays other monotheistic religions, such as Buddhism, Islam and Judaism.

Due to recent breakthroughs in physics,[11] the concepts of space and time proposed by Newton and introduced by Kant in his philosophy can now be unequivocally disproven (time differences between different parts of the world have been measured). Moreover, new theories about shifts in the laws of physics over time and their constant evolution, which is similar to Darwinian evolution, have challenged the long-standing position of theoretical physics on quantum gravity. Just as the universe is conceived in relational terms (all elements develop and grow interactively) from different perspectives – such as Smolin's secular and scientific perspective, as well as Rovelli's[12] and Molari's[13] perspectives – all religions as well as atheists must now adopt a *relational* approach focused on dialogue and mutually beneficial encounter. Such an approach should not consider difference and pluralism as an obstacle or a limitation to overcome or combat (such as with terrorist attacks), but as an inevitable reality which constitutes an opportunity for growth and common enrichment.

Of course, some of these ideas can also be found in your recent book, *Conversations About God and Man,*[14] written with the theologian and teacher at Warsaw, Stanislaw Obirek, as well as in the central thesis of your lectio magistralis held at the tenth edition of *Turin Spirituality*, in September 2014, whose topic was *the challenge of the "Smart Heart"*.[15] In these contexts, by reflecting on the quest for harmony between mind and spirit, you presented your reflections on God and Man and on the eternal quest for truth and you affirmed that there is no way to prove God's existence, "but our human existence results in the impossibility to reach that knowledge and in the necessity of living without it, also conscious of its absence". Moreover you state that human life is "on a wire", and morality is not the recipe for an easy life: "Forcing men to choose, they are exposed to the biggest temptation. God invited them to join him in the ongoing act of caring for creation".

At this stage, with respect to the clash of different religions, ethics and morals, I would like to know your opinion on the development of authoritarian and violent swerves as those mentioned above. Are there really religious differences or perhaps are we facing power struggles and violent attempts to manipulate and oppress other human beings? Apart from this, could you please clarify your position regarding religious pluralism and the chance for peaceful coexistence? The analysis of how to tackle these phenomena of violence would be interesting and compelling as well. Personally speaking, I think responding to violence with violence has never managed to resolve conflicts over the long term. The present situation requires establishing a relational and dialogue-based approach and not a hierarchical approach between the different opinions and points of view (obviously, the way anyone expresses his/her point of view must be kept within certain limits); perhaps, as it has been proposed, one solution would be setting up a kind of United Nations for religions, with arbiters who ensure that all parties play the game according to the standards of *fair play*.

Zygmunt Bauman: The great playwright and story-teller Antony Chekhov, known for his mastery of fishing crystal-clear logic out of the muddled waters of life's illogicality, appraised his fellow truth-seekers that if a gun is hanged on the wall in the first scene of a play, it must be fired in the third at the latest. By bringing that logic into view, Chekhov put his finger on one of the two major reasons for the spectacular incidents of violence to occupy ever more expanding space among realities and in the prevailing imagery of the present-day world. Courtesy of the cutting-edge while profits-greedy arms industry, whole-heartedly supported by high-GNP-figures politicians while evading their half-hearted attempts of controlling its order-books, guns hung on walls are nowadays aplenty, as never before, in the first scenes of most avidly played games. Even without Chekhov's wisdom we would be aware (and not allowed to forget) of living on a minefield saturated with explosives. And of minefields, we know that they are saturated with explosives, and so explosions are all but inevitable to occur; what we don't know is where and when.

The second logic contributing to the present-day explosion of violence derives from the meeting of their spectacularity with the cutting-edge, ratings-greedy and selling figures–greedy media industry. Pictures and stories of violence are among the most sellable offers of that industry – the more cruel, gory and blood-curdling the better. No wonder that media-managers love serving them as the coffee shop managers vie to advertise the coffee they serve: as fresh and hot. For the price of a gun whoever wishes to make himself visible world-wide can count, without miss, on impassioned and heartfelt cooperation of multi-billion-worth media; instantly and with no further effort one can lift even a relatively tiny and woefully local incident to the rank of a globally momentous, state-of-the-art, world-shattering event. Its echoes will reverberate for a long time to come; who knows, perhaps even change the course of history! Say what you will, this is an un-missable opportunity, a temptation which a budding terrorist worth his salt (as well as downtrodden and dejected, demeaned and humiliated youngsters drafted to the terrorist cause by their cunning and seasoned recruiters) is utterly unlikely to overlook. Seekers of fame may rest assured that this society of ours, notorious for its inhospitality to nice and decent people, is un-precedentedly hospitable to the heirs of Herostratus.

The two logics sketched briefly above are not, obviously, the *causes* of the phenomenon you wish us to consider. Neither form they, singly or together, its *sufficient condition*. But they constitute, when combined, its *necessary condition*. Without them being both present and acting in tandem, the outburst of violence in its present shape and form would've been all but inconceivable.

And so we have arrived, dear Agostino, to a point of contention between us, while attempting in unison to understand the same bizarre departure we currently witness: a departure that contravenes (some would go as far as saying: disproves) the high hopes of *les philosophes* who two to three centuries ago put their wager on the universalizing capacity of Reason and Enlightenment: those, as they believed (wrongly, as it now seems), twin vehicles of the civilizing process. I suspect in your presentation of "*religious* fundamentalism" and (after Huntington) "war of *civilizations*" the fallacy of taking form for the substance, wrappings for contents, effects for causes – all in all, an interpretation for its object. I strongly believe that the current rise in the volume and reach of violence needs be seen against the background of the massive production of human misery: humiliation, denial of life prospects together with human dignity – and their only-to-be-expected outcome: seething lust for vengeance. Terrorism, of which we need to expect more yet to come, however eagerly the governments flex their muscle to tame it and subdue, is – we might say – the weapon of the disarmed, a power of the disempowered. And it will remain such – as long as the agony and grief of having been excluded, or of living one's life under the threat of exclusion, will go on rising unabated as they presently are. With this challenge to human dignity (and in a rising scale to the very survival) persisting, it would be naïve to the core to suppose that the seekers of conscripts to the suicide bombing will return from their recruiting hassle empty-handed, under whatever banner they propose the prospective suicide bombers to rally.

It was Pope Francis who recently, the sole among the public figures in global limelight, reached to the roots of our present predicament (in his Apostolic Exhortation Evangelii Gaudium), reminding us that:

> it is a matter of hearing the cry of entire peoples, the poorest peoples of the earth, since "peace is founded not only on respect for human rights, but also on respect for the rights of peoples". Sadly, even human rights can be used as a justification for an inordinate defense of individual rights or the rights of the richer peoples. With due respect for the autonomy and culture of every nation, we must never forget that the planet belongs to all mankind and is meant for all mankind; the mere fact that some people are born in places with fewer resources or less development does not justify the fact that they are living with less dignity. It must be reiterated that "the more fortunate should renounce some of their rights so as to place their goods more generously at the service of others". To speak properly of our own rights, we need to

broaden our perspective and to hear the plea of other peoples and other regions than those of our own country. We need to grow in a solidarity which "would allow all peoples to become the artisans of their destiny", since "every person is called to self-fulfilment".

He also pointed to the way – by no means easy, yet the only promising one – leading out of the evil and menacing condition in which we've cast ourselves by plugging our ears to that "cry of entire peoples":

> The need to resolve the structural causes of poverty cannot be delayed, not only for the pragmatic reason of its urgency for the good order of society, but because society needs to be cured of a sickness which is weakening and frustrating it, and which can only lead to new crises. Welfare projects, which meet certain urgent needs, should be considered merely temporary responses. As long as the problems of the poor are not radically resolved by rejecting the absolute autonomy of markets and financial speculation and by attacking the structural causes of inequality, no solution will be found for the world's problems or, for that matter, to any problems. Inequality is the root of social ills.

We can no longer trust in the unseen forces and the invisible hand of the market. Growth in justice requires more than economic growth, while presupposing such growth: it requires decisions, programmes, mechanisms and processes specifically geared to a better distribution of income, the creation of sources of employment and an integral promotion of the poor which goes beyond a simple welfare mentality. I am far from proposing an irresponsible populism, but the economy can no longer turn to remedies that are a new poison, such as attempting to increase profits by reducing the work force and thereby adding to the ranks of the excluded.

Shifting the blame for the society that rejects, and for all practical intents and purposes makes null and void the human – all too human – impulse of "mutual aid and solidarity" onto "laicism and moral relativism" is but a stratagem deployed by unscrupulous demagogues, whether of religious or any other denomination, away from its genuine causes so vividly and lucidly described by Pope Francis. The sufferings of the demeaned, degraded, deprived and excluded victims could be "extra-systemic": they might be strikingly similar regardless of the specificity of the particular "order", and the "discipline" it demands, by which they have been caused. The trick is how to use, fraudulently, the capital of human wrath and vengefulness stored by the wrongs committed by one "system" onto another in the on-going inter-systemic strife. The borders have been already pre-drawn by the apostles, priests and preachers of the antagonistic monotheisms, and as the great Norwegian anthropologist Fredrik Barth teaches, once the borders have been drawn the difference justifying drawing them are eagerly sought and found or invented. "Their" (people on the other side of the border) "laicism and moral relativism", all but innocent of causing our rebellion-prompting misery, are one of such "differences" conveniently charged with responsibility for the anguish and presented as the main (perhaps even the sole) obstacle to the restoration of justice as well as of "mutual aid and solidarity".

I fully agree with you that "the believer, but also the layman or the atheist, cannot avoid thinking that all other people's faiths or non-faiths are wrong. Conflict, therefore, seems inevitable". Religious variety of fundamentalism plays an extraordinarily prominent role in framing the stage on which the game of conflicts is played – under conditions of coexistence of monotheism entrenched since the 1648 Westphalian settlement ("cuius regio eius religio", with the "natio" substituted two centuries later for "religio") in their respective state borders (and states, according Max Weber's memorable definition, remaining in theory and ambition, though no longer in practice, formations claiming monopoly on the means of coercion).

There is a paradox endemic to a monotheist creed: it insists that God of its choice is one and only – though by the very fact of persistently reiterating that assertion it obliquely admits the presence of that God's contenders. Because of that paradox, monotheistic religion cannot but be constantly ready for the fray; bristling with bayonets, combative and belligerent in confrontation with alternative (false, as it is bound to aver) pretenders to God's status. Monotheistic faith is by its nature militant and in a state of a permanent enmity and intermittent war – hot or cold – with the world outside its realm; it is viewed for that reason as a particularly tempting, indeed favourite, choice for warriors of great variety of causes – especially the most intransigent and ruthless among them. After all, all stops can be pulled out in a fight waged by the devoted to the Church in the name of *one and only* God against His enemies. Once you know that in hoc signo vinces – you can, and you will, catch as you catch can. The popular, though questionable quote from Dostoievsky suggests that "if God does not exist, everything is permitted". Closer to the facts of life, though alas yet more portending, is to conclude that if there is one and only God, everything done in His name to His detractors, however cruel, goes". No doubt equals no scruples.

The principle of "cuius regio eius religio" binds no longer our globalized and diasporized world. There are streets in densely populated London where Catholic and protestant Churches, Sunnite and Shiite mosques as well as orthodox and reform synagogues are erected just a few dozen yards from each other. Men and women of different faiths – heathens, heretics, dissenters or whatever other derogatory, stigmatizing or condemnatory names might be used to brand them – are no longer distant and misty creatures in seldom- or never-visited foreign lands, but next-door neighbours, work-mates, fathers and mothers of our children's school friends; at any rate, the daily, all-too-frequent sights at the crowded city streets and squares. Mutual separation is no longer on the cards, however passionately we might try. Monotheistic gods are doomed to live in close proximity of each other on our incurably polytheistic planet; indeed, in each other's company. Huntington's vision of the war of civilization waged in the planetary space does not descend to the urban level; at that level, as I tried repeatedly to show, mixophilia fights for the better with mixophobia. Willy-nilly, knowingly or not, by design or by default, ways and means of living daily in peace, even in collaboration with difference, are invented, experimented with, put to a test and adopted.

Notes

1 *Independent,* April 21, 2016.
2 ICIR International Center for Investigative Reporting. "The Figures that Show Boko Haram Was Stronger in 2017 than in 2016." Accessed January 25, 2018. https://www.icirnigeria.org/the-figures-that-show-boko-haram-was-stronger-in-2017-than-in-2016/
3 Ibid., pp. 28–42.
4 Ibid., pp. 135–136.
5 Ibid., p. 479.
6 Cfr. A. Portera, "The Religious Education in a Pluralistic and Multicultural Society", in *Self-investigation and Transcendence: Psychological Approaches to the Religious Identity in a Pluralistic Society,* eds. M. Aletti and G. Rossi (Turin: Centro Scientifico Editore, 1999), pp. 317–324.
7 "The ecumenical movement includes the activities and the initiatives that, according to the different necessities of the church and the current opportunities, have been created and intended in order to promote Christian unity. First of all, all the efforts to eliminate words, judgments and works that do not reflect in a fair and true way the conditions of separated brothers and therefore make the mutual relationships with them more difficult; then the dialogue between properly prepared experts in the meetings that take place between Christians of the different churches and communities with religious purposes, where everyone explains the doctrine of his/her own community and clearly presents its characteristics" (*Unitatis redintegratio,* November 21, 1964).
8 "As the spiritual heritage common to Christians and Jews is so big, this holy and sacred Synod wants to foster and recommend a mutual

knowledge and respect that can be gained especially with biblical and theological studies and with a fraternal dialogue" (*Nostra aetate,* November 28, 1965).

9 c) "And although, throughout the centuries, several disagreements and enmities have emerged between Christians and Muslims, the holy and sacred Synod urges you all to forget the past and sincerely practice the mutual understanding, as well as to defend and promote together, for all human beings, social justice, moral values, peace and freedom" (Ibid.).

10 "Moreover, although the church totally opposes atheism, it sincerely recognizes that all men, believers and non-believers, must contribute to the building of the world in which they all live: this, of course, can't be achieved without a sincere and cautious dialogue. Moreover, the church deplores the discrimination between believers and non-believers that some civil authorities unfairly introduce, as they don't want to recognize people's fundamental rights" (*Gaudium et spes,* December 7, 1965).

11 L. Smolin, *Time Reborn* (Turin: Einaudi, 2014).

12 C. Rovelli, *La realtà non è ciò che appare (Reality is Not What it Seems)* (Milan: Raffaello Cortina, 2014).

13 C. Molari, *Teologia del pluralismo religioso (Theology of Religious Pluralism)* (Rome: Pazzini, 2012).

14 Zygmunt Bauman, *Conversazioni su Dio e sull'uomo* (Roma-Bari: Laterza, 2014).

15 L. Tortello, "Bauman Talks of God but Doesn't Know if it Exists," *La Stampa,* September 24, 2014.

3 Pollution and loss of biodiversity

Is the human species at risk of extinction?

Zygmunt Bauman and Agostino Portera

Agostino Portera: In addition to the issue of dialogue between faiths and religions, another major challenge of our times concerns the environment. In light of the most recent scientific data regarding the health of our planet, a troubling picture emerges, which I would like to consider together with you.

In his book *The Crisis of Biological Diversity* (published in 1985), the world's leading authority on biodiversity, emeritus Professor of Biology at Harvard, Edward O. Wilson, regarded as one of the first theorists to develop the concept of "biodiversity", underlines the fact that in the 1980s the best scientific evidence produced an estimate of 1.4 million species of animals and plants on the planet. Most of the animals were insects. Nowadays, thanks to an improvement in research technology, researchers estimate the number to be 1.8 million, with an increase of about 400,000 species, most of which are insects. Biologists have found living beings in boiling hot springs thousands of feet below the ocean surface and nestled under thousands of feet of ice. Including more accessible but incompletely explored places such as tropical rain forests, the number could rise to 10 million. Adding bacteria, fungi and other microbes, the number of species may rise to 100 million. Although for human beings variety is of crucial importance, in our "liquid-modern" time, biodiversity seems to be experiencing a profound crisis, the consequence of which is the loss of many of the biological "genetic encyclopaedias" that have been created over millions of years (it takes about 10 million years for the planet to reach the same level of biological diversity after a die-off).

In a subsequent analysis,[1] Wilson also stresses the thesis that the loss or erosion of ecosystems has caused real tragedies: the destabilization of links in food chains due to extinction; the loss of opportunities in medicine, biotechnology and agriculture; and, last but not least, the permanent loss of major parts of national and global natural heritage.

Citing data from over 10,000 scientists in the World Conservation Union, he shows that 51% of known reptiles, 52% of known insects, and 73% of known flowering plants, as well as many mammals, birds and amphibians, are currently in danger of extinction. Some species will probably become extinct even before being discovered, before any medicinal use or other scientific contributions can be assessed. For example: since 1960 the number of racing pigeons has dropped from hundreds of millions to zero; Haiti has destroyed about 99% of its forests and polluted all its watercourses; 47 out of the 51 species of amphibians are in danger of extinction; 32.5% of all amphibians are at risk of extinction as well as 12% of reptiles; 23% of mammals and the same percentage of birds are at risk of extinction; in China, 80% of the 50,000 km of the largest watercourses no longer contain fish; Australia's Great Barrier Coral Reef has halved in size in the last 40 years; the rate of extinction in freshwater ecosystems is 100 times higher than before the appearance of Homo Sapiens. The cause of this irreversible decline of biodiversity, Wilson explains, can be summarized in the acronym HIPPO: habitat loss, invasive species (foreign harmful species, introduced in some areas that replace other species), pollution, population (overpopulation) and overharvesting (over exploitation through hunting, fishing and harvesting). All of these factors, which often potentiate one another, are related to human beings.

Nowadays all of humanity is facing a growing challenge with air, water and ground contamination. Scientific data[2] show that air *pollution* represents a growing problem, especially in urban areas. The main causes are believed to be industrialization, urban sprawl and the increase in toxic emissions from the combustion of fossil fuels. Although the effects are also due to natural events, such as earthquakes and volcanic eruptions, most of the known air pollutants are mostly consequences of human activities, such as road traffic, industrial and photochemical smog, as well as emissions caused by accidents such as at chemical and nuclear plants or forest fires. A case in point is the "Terra dei Fuochi", Land of Fires, in the province of Caserta in Italy, where organized criminals have illegally buried highly toxic waste (and often burn it to make more space). These criminals are polluting the ground where they and their children live and are making it harmful for future generations. Another pressing issue is the *greenhouse effect*. The heat balance of our planet is affected by solar radiation and by heat energy that is absorbed and reflected by the earth's surface and by the gases in the different layers of the atmosphere. The naturally occurring greenhouse gas emissions guarantee the maintenance of the average temperature level of earth's surface, estimated to be around 15°C. According to some scientists,[3] in the last two centuries excess greenhouse gas emissions (especially carbon dioxide) produced by human activities have given rise to an increase of about 1.5 W/m^2 in heat energy, resulting in a global warming of about 0.6°C. In the last 40 years, increase in the atmospheric CO2 concentration has been particularly high (around 15%). Water pollution, due to the release of urban waste (food, detergents, plastics, mineral oils, asphalt), rural waste (fertilizers, plant protection products, pesticides) and industrial waste (heavy metals, chlorides) into the environment, is becoming more problematic as well. Such waste has recently created the "Pacific Trash Vortex", which is an island of trash, especially plastic, that has formed in the Pacific Ocean since the 1950s, with a diameter of about 2,500 km, a surface of 4,909,000 km², a depth of 30 metres and a weight of 3,500,000 tons. Another area of particular importance, related to pollution, is *food waste*. According to FAO[4] data, although 870 million people currently suffer from hunger, a third of the world food production is thrown to waste (80% of which is still edible). Every year 1.3 billion tons of food (worth 750 billion dollars) are wasted, and their disposal causes pollution: 170 million tons of carbon dioxide every year, in addition to excess water consumption and soil degradation. The Italian population seems to be particularly involved in this phenomenon. Every citizen throws away on average 146 kg of food every year. Especially household (42%) and food waste (14%) are excessive, but also production (13%), processing (26%) and retail waste (5%).

Given these facts and trends, serious reflection is necessary. In my opinion, a planet in which animals and plants are killed and destroyed in order to preserve the superfluous material things of another species (the human species, especially in very industrialized countries) is unsustainable; a society in which a printer toner is more expensive than a printer and a mobile phone battery is more expensive than a mobile phone is untenable; a society based on the mass disposal of industrial and food waste (not to mention the waste of time, energy and resources that many goods require) is shaky. Pierre Rabhi,[5] a farmer from Algeria, who is now living in France, explains very clearly the problem of pollution in agriculture. He explains that the situation began to worsen when agricultural activity was linked to the price of oil. Since the horse was replaced with "horse power", the equilibrium of agriculture with the earth, which had been sustainable for millennia, has been lost, and the use of monocultures, herbicides, pesticides, non-reproducible seeds, etc., have increased. For the farmer, who now sits in his (air conditioned) tractor cab as opposed to working the fields with his bare hands, profit has become the main priority, to the detriment of the health of the earth, the plants and – consequently – also the men and women who produce and/or consume agricultural products. Rabhi reveals that nowadays 12 calories of crude oil are necessary to produce one calorie of food; due to increasingly low prices; in the so-called civilized countries food only represents 15% of the economy, less than the cost of medicines. Planet earth seems to "suffer from mankind". Although humans are relatively new on earth, and among the physically weakest species, due to their intelligence, women and men have turned into "predators without predators" and have established absolute dominion over the whole planet and all living species. In his opinion, the human species now represents "an ecological disaster of colossal magnitude". The land division of the planet into nation-states and the drawing of national borders only perpetuate insecurities and contribute to arms races, wars and destruction rather than protecting the citizens and fostering prosperity.

You also deal with this subject in the book *On Education,*[6] written with Riccardo Mazzeo, in which you assert that liquid modernity is characterized by "the ghost of the superfluous things". We are living in a civility of excess, superabundance and waste, a society defined by ephemerality, volatility and precariousness. We are "hungry for objects", and driven by consumerism. We behave in an egoistic and materialistic way.

In this context, I think, a further reflection on the gravity of current dangers is necessary. The earth was formed around 4.54 billion years ago, multi-cellular life and animals appeared for 600–750 million years and the species of homo sapiens first began to evolve since nearly 200,000 years. In the third millennium, the central challenge is not only to protect endangered species of insects (we are all too happy to kill mosqui; however, bees' death means the end of the pollination cycle and of life: the existence of humanity itself is at risk). The human species is at risk of going extinct. Earth and many living species have been able to live without humans for million years. After the extinction of the dinosaurs, humans eventually emerged as the dominant species. Life will certainly continue to exist on earth even if human beings become extinct. Perhaps the era of mice or cockroaches will start.

Zygmunt Bauman: Possibility of such an era impending is not a figment of imagination. It happened already in the past, even if not as yet on the global scale. One of the relatively well recorded cases is that of Easter Island, an isolated piece of land amidst the largest ocean on Earth (more than 2,000 km distant from another – almost uninhabited

– Pitcairn Island, and more than 3,500 km from the South-American continent) once self-sufficient and economically and culturally thriving from the time of the first human settlements established in the course of the first millenium, which, however, by the time of European arrival in 1722 saw its population dropping to 2,000–3,000 from about 15,000 a mere century earlier.[7] The main culprit and immediate cause of that catastrophe was overharvesting and overhunting resulting in deforestation of the island, followed in turn by the erosion of the topsoil. Twenty-one species of trees and all bird populations had become extinct.[8] In the light of the facts you've collated from all parts of the globe, the sad fate of Easter Island may well be viewed as a local rehearsal of a forthcoming global production of the drama.

In his new book[9] Arne Johan Vetlesen, a remarkable Norwegian philosopher, confronts point-blank the task of the "further reflection on the gravity of current dangers" which you, so rightly, postulate; doing so, he strengthens yet more your case – reaching to the roots of the present trouble by pointing out that "the longer nature is treated as a mere means to human-centred ends, the more degraded it will become. And the more degraded nature becomes, the more of an uphill struggle will be to make the argument – however impressive in theory – that nature possesses intrinsic value". We have landed in a sort of a vicious circle. Short of a radical reversal of trend and profound revision of our hegemonic philosophy and our mode of life, we are confronted with a challenge no less daunting and arduous than the untying of the proverbial Gordian knot. It so happened and continues to happen, that in a stark opposition to popular hopes the departures in scientific knowledge and technological know-how which we dub summarily "the progress" are cutting under very conditions of human collective survival. As Vetlesen puts it:

> The less there actually exists of nature *qua* unexplored, unknown, unexploited, the more the cosmologies fashioned by the sense of powerlessness come to lose their hold. The shift, then, is from being at the mercy of nature and all the nonhuman lifeforms and species it consists of, to commanding what demonstrably is increasingly growing control and mastery over it, principally by way of a wave of new technologies immensely more efficient than those predating them. *"Extractivism"* is Naomi Klein's apt term for the still dominant paradigm: "a nonreciprocal, dominance-based relationship with the earth, one purely of taking",[10] working *against* rather than with the flow, rhythms, and regenerational dynamics and capacities of nature.[11]

And then Vetlesen[12] quotes Teresa Brennan[13]:

> Capital plays God and redirects nature at its own speed and from its own subject-centered standpoint. It is playing with high stakes here, because it is literally altering the *physis* of the world, adjusting the inbuilt logic of nature and the spatio-temporal continuum to suit itself. [...] It establishes its own foundation, but it does so by consuming the real foundations, the logic of natural substances.

Brennan and her contemporaries had their predecessors – the most noteworthy and perhaps the most influential between them having been Lewis Mumford.[14] Well before the current explosion of "sustainability" concerns and studies, even before the very concept of the "sustainability of the planet" was coined, Mumford elaborated two ideal-typical attitudes to non-human nature and their underlying philosophies, related respectively to agriculture (confined to its pre-industrialization history) and mining (in the form coming to full maturity in the middle of the 19th century):

> Agriculture creates balance between wild nature and man's social needs. It returns deliberately what man subtracts from the earth; while the ploughed field, the trim orchard, the serried vineyard, the vegetables, the grains, the flowers, are all examples of disciplined purpose, orderly growth, and beautiful form. The process of mining, on the other hand, is destructive: the immediate product of mining is disorganized and inorganic; and what is once taken out of the quarry or the pithead cannot be replaced. Add to this the fact that continuing occupation in agriculture brings cumulative improvement of the landscape and a finer adaptation of it to human needs; while mines as a rule pass quickly from riches to exhaustion, from exhaustion to desertion, often within a few generations. Mining thus presents the very image of human discontinuity, have today and gone tomorrow, now feverish with gain, now depleted and vacant.

In our age lived under the rule of technology developing its own developmental logic and own momentum, the earth, as Martin Heidegger noted, reveals itself as "[only] a coal mining district, [its] soil as a mineral deposit"; it is left entirely to the wind's blowing. But the windmill does not unlock energy from the air currents in order to store it. In contrast, a tract of land is challenged into the putting out of coal and ore. The earth now reveals itself as a coal mining district, the soil as a mineral deposit. The field that the peasant formerly cultivated and set in order [*bestellte*] appears differently than it did when to set in order still meant to take care of and to maintain. The work of the peasant does not challenge the soil of the field. In the sowing of the grain it places the seed in the keeping of the forces of growth and watches over its increase.[15]

So you do have, dear Agostino, a strong case – but so did all those above-quoted authors, as well as lots of others here unnamed, though all of them reputable and widely read. The facts you've garnered speak for themselves, and conclusions you draw are thoroughly convincing; but there are little (or at least far too few) signs that are given the attention which their import and gravity require. We may have recently talked and wrote more than before on the dangers that threaten sustainability of our planet and so also of the prospects of our collective survival. But our deeds did not follow the words to however many addressed and at however level of power and influence spoken. Our collective consciousness must yet as it seems cover a lot of distance in order to reach our collective conscience and through it beget an adequate collective action. We may talk and think differently than we did a few decades ago, but our way of daily life, and our hierarchy of preferences in particular, have hardly twitched; if anything, their ominous, doomful proclivities have acquired their own self-reinforcing momentum.

In 1975–1976 Elias Canetti collected a number of his essays, written within a 26-years long time span, in a volume entitled *Das Gewissen der Worte* – "Conscience of words"; the volume closes with the speech on the profession of writer, delivered by Canetti in January 1976 in Munich. In it, he confronts the question whether, in the present world situation, "there is something to which writers or people heretofore thought to be writers could be of use". To explain what sort of a writer he has in mind, he quotes a statement made by an unknown author on 23 August 1939: "It's over. Were I a real writer, I should've been able to prevent the war"; the author of these words insists that writer is "real" in as far as her or his words make a difference between well-being and catastrophe. What makes writers "real" is the impact of their words on reality; in Canetti's rendition, "desire to assume responsibility for everything that can be expressed in words, and to do penance for their, the words', failure". To leave no room for taking his opinion lightly as referring to grave, yet fortunately past, events, he emphasizes that the menace has lost nothing of its topicality: "there are no writers today, but we ought to passionately desire that they be [...] In a world, which one would most willingly define as the blindest of worlds, the presence of people who nevertheless insist on the possibility of its change acquires supreme importance".

Our world seems to be anything but hospitable to the "real writers" as described by Canetti. It appears to be well protected not against catastrophes, but against their few and far between prophets – while most of us, the residents of that well protected world, are well protected against listening to the few voices crying in their respective wildernesses – at least as long as the right to residence is not yet to us brusquely denied, as it is bound to be in not-so-distant a future if our contrived deafness persists. As another great intellectual of yore, Arthur Koestler, kept reminding us: on the eve of another catastrophe, "in 1933 and during the next two or three years, the only people with an intimate understanding of what went on in the young Third Reich were a few thousand refugees"; a distinction that condemned them to the "always unpopular, shrill-voiced part of Cassandra". Koestler's own conclusion was sombre: "Amos, Hosea, Jeremiah, were pretty good propagandists, and yet failed to shake their people and to warn them. Cassandra's voice was said to have pierced walls, and yet the Trojan war took place".

It seems that one needs catastrophes to happen in order to recognize and admit their coming. A chilling thought, if there ever was one ...

Notes

1 E. O. Wilson, *The Creation: An Appeal to Save Life on Earth* (New York: W.W. Norton & Company, 2006).
2 J. H. Seinfeld, S.N. Pandies, *Atmospheric Chemistry and Physics: From Air Pollution to Climate Change* (New York: Wiley, 1998).
3 R. P. Schwarzenbach, P.M. Gschewend, D.M. Imboden, *Environmental Organic Chemistry* (New York: Wiley, 2003).
4 FAO, *Food and Nutrition in Number 2014* (Rome: Food and Agriculture Organization of the United Nations, 2014).
5 P. Rabhi, *Manifeste pour la Terre e pour l'Humanisme* (Arles: Actes Sud, 2008) (2011 add editore torino).
6 Z. Bauman, R. Mazzeo, *On Education* (Cambridge: Polity Press, 2012).
7 As estimated by Barbara A. West, *Encyclopedia of the Peoples of Asia and Oceania* (New York: Infobase Publishing, 2008), p. 684.
8 http://en.wikipedia.org/wiki/Easter_Island#
9 Arne Johan Vetlesen, *Denial of Nature: Environmental Philosophy in the Era of Global Capitalism* (Milton Park: Routledge, 2015), p. 2.
10 Naomi Klein, *This Changes Everything: Capitalism vs. the Climate* (London: Allen Lane, 2014), p. 169.
11 Arne Johan Vetlesen, *Denial of Nature: Environmental Philosophy in the Era of Global Capitalism* (Milton Park: Routledge, 2015), pp. 16–17
12 Ibid., p. 41

13 Teresa Brennan, *Exhausting Modernity: Grounds for a New Economy* (Milton Park: Routledge, 2000), p. 131.

14 See in particular Lewis Mumford, *The City in History* (San Diego: Harcourt, Brace & World, 1961).

15 Ibid., pp. 450–451. See Heidegger's "The Question Concerning Technology". Here quoted after http://simondon.ocular-witness.com/wp-content/uploads/2008/05/question_concerning_technology.pdf

4 Identity in a time of glocalization and liquid modernity

Zygmunt Bauman and Agostino Portera

Agostino Portera: The many changes that characterize our times not only concern the environment or the cultural dimension of groups of people and society, but also the most intimate part of every human being. Therefore, I would like to reflect with you on a topic that is very dear to you and me, that is the theme of personal identity. I am aware that you have already widely dealt with this concept in many publications, but I'd like to put it on the agenda again.

The increasing redrawing of national borders (for example, the European Union, the former Yugoslavia, the Soviet Union) and the constant boost in (real and virtual) geographic mobility influence the culture and the identities of human beings in many positive and negative ways (some of which have already been mentioned in this book). The new challenge for people with different cultural origins is to find a way to coexist in increasingly multicultural societies, in a time of globalization and "liquid modernity". Nowadays, one of the most demanding issues is the effects such changes have on identity construction. Do enculturation and acculturation, or living and growing up in a bi- or multicultural context and society necessarily imply an exacerbation of conflict and disruption, or may they offer many positive opportunities which can lead to enhanced personal and social development?

To this end, Erik Erikson could offer great insight to our reflections, since he is one of the first and most prominent researchers, arguably the "discoverer", of the question of identity building in the scientific field. He not only lived the multicultural and migratory experience himself, being a German-born Danish Jew who fled to the United States after Hitler's rise to power, but also did many empirical studies of American society as well as the so-called subcultures or minority groups (for example, Native American tribes). In the formulation of his theories, Erikson[1] defines identity as a specific synthesis, as an integrative process of the self, as an activity that involves psychological as well as social aspects. At the end of his research, he developed an epigenetic model of human development, divided into eight life stages, each of them characterized by an evolutionary crisis with specific challenges. In the case of an appropriate response and conflict re-solution, the person is able to advance to the next life stage and strengthen his/her own personality; in the case of a failure to resolve the challenge, stagnation or disorder occurs. During the first stage the person must acquire basic trust in the world around him/her, which will be essential for life; during the second stage he/she must achieve autonomy, by overcoming doubt and shame; during the third stage (towards the end of the third year of life and corresponding to the genital stage in Freudian theory) the person must take actions to overcome his/her sense of guilt; and during the fourth stage he/she must overcome inferiority and begin to demonstrate industry. According to Erikson, adolescence corresponds to the fifth stage – identity versus role confusion – and is marked by the transition from childhood to adulthood, during which the person seeks individuals and ideas he/she can trust, by seeking out roles in life for which he/she must not feel ashamed. In his opinion, if the young teenager can overcome the crises of the first five stages, he/she will be able to construct a healthy and stable personal identity, which will protect him/her from role conflicts and identity crises; he/she will move towards a profession and assimilate ideologies that ensure recognition and confirmation from peers and parents. According to this model,[2] if the subject does not develop a stable and well-established personal identity, and the identity crisis of adolescence is prolonged, a stage of "identity confu-sion" occurs during which socially deviant behaviour and/or mental disorders may ensue.[3]

Does this theory, formulated in the 1970s and based on mono-cultural societies, assume the same value today, in a time of globali-zation and complexity?

Personally, I do not think so. The dramatic changes resulting from globalization inevitably cause profound changes that also concern personal and social identity. Where in the past human life was gen-erally marked by specific stages, rules and inhibitions imposed by tradition, religion or the state, nowadays (especially in industrialized societies) identity is defined by the constant choices of a person. Ulrich Beck[4] talks about "choice biography and do-it-yourself biography" that, depending on the decisions an individual makes, can turn into "success biography" or "risk biography". He considers the human being to be *homo complexus*, who is, like *homo optionis*, condemned to live without certainties and solid points of reference for the formation of values, faces the issue of modern citizen education in relation to his/her identity. Nowadays, instead of strong and axiologically rooted identities, there is an assembly work or *Patchwork*, where single components or cultural standards are not always in harmony with the previously acquired components, where the uncertainty and the principles of outward appearance (show) and of change (flexibility, ductility) sometimes exceed the components linked to the inwardness and therefore endanger the psychological stability. Since the end of the Cold War, Western society has had to deal with a more and more complex, as well as uncertain and dangerous, world that, according to Beck's definition, has turned into a *Risikogesellschaft* (risk society).

In one of your many books,[5] you likewise talk about how liquid modernity has caused significant changes concerning personal and social identity. Nowadays, the fragmentary, discontinuous and superficial nature of human contact is a typical element of interpersonal relations. The traditional social stability is falling apart ever more rapidly, and parental and social relationships are weakening, constantly challenged by the satisfaction of individual needs. Amongst human beings a slow, but inexorable dispersion of social competences is taking place; personal and social identity is increasingly dependent on the market and inevitably reflects the market's extremely uncertain and unstable nature. Likewise,[6] in a more recent work on identity,[7] you describe how human beings are not able to stop and stand still in a time of liquid modernity: time prevails over space. Today the perception of one's own identity has completely changed as a result of the crisis of the systems of belonging and inclusion caused by the transport revolution and the weakening (and sometimes disintegration) of the local community structures. While in the past (in the pre-modern experience of proximity and of networks of familiarity, men and women didn't have to face the problem of individuality) the nation-state strove to foster the construction of a national identity within its own territorial borders, since the crisis of the nation-state, personal identity has lost its reference points in the frameworks of society and tradition (gender, country or place of birth, family, social class) that once made them seem and feel "natural", pre-determined and non-negotiable. Especially young people, who try to be part of a "group", are often involved in electronically mediated, fragile, virtual networks, which are easy to join and leave. As you properly state, in a time of globalization, because "the State can't and doesn't want to protect its marriage with the society anymore",[8] many scenarios have appeared: (a) people who can construct and reconstruct their identities more or less as they like, drawing upon the huge well of options in the world; (b) people who cannot adopt the identity they would like, and who cannot express their preferences, but have to accept the burden of an identity imposed by others; (c) people who are being denied the right to claim a distinct identity (this group corresponds to people defined as the "subclass": homeless, beggars, refugees). While in the past identity was primarily determined by one's productive role in the division of labour and the state was the guarantor, nowadays the state is no longer a reliable fulfiller of the demands of citizens, who are often obsessed with the fear of being excluded. Following the "liquefaction" of social structures and institutions during early modernity, when personal identity was determined by birth, identities are now defined by the tasks individuals have to carry out during their biography and career paths. Like Beck, you point out how in the present men and women build their own identities using pieces of a puzzle, without knowing in advance the final picture. Similar to a piece of visual *bricolage*, the artist only uses the material available, and starting from a certain amount of pieces, organizes and puts them together to obtain satisfactory images, in relation to the temporary purposes.

In an attempt to understand the question about the construction of personal and social identity in a time of migration and cultural complexity, in the 1990s I carried out a detailed empirical study,[9] a longitudinal qualitative case study, using semi-structured interviews. I analyzed the life-stories, conflicts, crises, problem-solving strategies and protective factors occurring among young people of Italian origin, living in southern Germany or southern Italy (after migration) for a period of up to seven years. The main purpose was to find an answer to the question of whether, with specific regard to identity construction, migration and life in a multicultural context represent a risk which leads to discomfort and illness, or whether they represent a positive influence with possibilities for personal enrichment and growth. The aim was to identify positive outcomes and opportunities, as well as negative outcomes and risks relating to migration and life in a multicultural context. The results largely confirmed the hypothesis that migration limited the fulfilment of some of the primary needs of young people who underwent bi-cultural or multi-cultural enculturation/acculturation.[10] The likelihood of success through adequate coping strategies or compensatory reactions was strongly reduced, mainly because of the differences between the parents' and the host country's value systems. On the basis of the results, some risk factors were identified that relate to the process of identity construction in a multicultural context. They include sudden, unprepared separation;

commuting (families that keep moving back-and-forth between home and host country); ambivalent behaviour (cultural differences between family and school: parents often push their children to passivity or submission to adults, while teachers encourage children to be active, inquisitive and independent); social marginality (financial problems, debt, the loss of social status and insufficient legal protection); discrimination; loneliness and language problems. In addition to the negative aspects, which led to pronounced crises and sometimes to disorders, the research also highlighted some protective factors which had a positive effect on the subjects' ability to face a crisis and cope with it and which in many cases also contributed to positive personal development and the construction of a positive and stable identity. The most important factors were: the establishment of a secure relationship with a caregiver during one's childhood (not necessarily with the mother); the parents' openness towards German society and culture; the parents' understanding and trust; the subject's readiness for separation; the subject's positive experience of acceptance and respect in the host country; teachers' and educators' understanding; a lack of pressure in or out of school to assimilate; and the role of friends as a "bridge" between different cultures. In short, the research clearly demonstrated that, despite many concrete obstacles (parents unemployment, marginalization, discrimination, inadequate housing situation), parents as well as teachers adopt mono-cultural strategies and are still unprepared to face multicultural situations, and the conflicting senses of belonging and multiple identities witnessed among children and adolescents. Forcing assimilation proved to be their greatest mistake.

The study also showed that the young people who could appropriate positive personal and social identities and who could benefit the most from living in a multicultural context (without destructive crises and mental or psychosomatic disorder), were not – as Erikson supposed – people with a strong culturally rooted identity, but people who (thanks to appropriate educational support and/or adequate coping strategies) were able to acquire an identity that I have defined, "intercultural". I use the term "intercultural identity" to describe people who have adopted a dialogic and interactive approach to both within themselves (between all the interiorized different cultural standards) as well as towards the significant people (peers and adults) they have lived with or encountered.

Therefore, in my opinion, in a time of liquid modernity, what needs to be promoted as the "healthiest" identity cannot be a mono-cultural identity, but an intercultural identity that is open (capable and willing) to adapt to constant change, a strong and stable identity that displays "humility" when confronted with diversity and otherness. The children of glocalization (according to Derrida,[11] we are living in a local world that is greatly influenced by global decisions) and global inter-dependence have to establish identities in compliance with the kalei-doscopic nature of their external reality (constant potential for cultural encounter and cultural shifts). In the third millennium, citizens should not be coerced to define themselves in nationalistic terms (the nation-state no longer corresponds – nor did it ever – to a single culture), but should be free to define themselves based upon their multiple affilia-tions and identifications (woman, interest for classical music, vege-tarian, football lover, political affiliation, religion, etc.). At the same time the challenge is to avoid the construction of "liquid" or "fluctu-ating" identities (as you rightfully state). Liquid modernity necessitates a *dynamic* identity, which embraces a state of constant change and learns to sort through many options (recognizing the risks and the opportunities) to carefully and continuously choose and, as needed, modify, attributes which are developmentally appropriate and which foster stability. I define these identities as *intercultural*, so as to em-phasize both their dynamism and their faculty to manage stereotypes and prejudices by effectively engaging both external and internal otherness (that is, their ability to avoid the risk of becoming too rigid or becoming foreign to oneself).

Zygmunt Bauman: You said it all; all that needs to be said about the issue of identity in times in which – to quote Michael Buravoy's 2014 presidential address to the International Sociological Association – instead of global labour movement we face the global movement of labour; and the consequences of the latter – crisscrossing archipela-goes of diasporas from the bird's eye perspective, and multiculturality of each and any habitat as perceived by rising number of human eyes (particularly in cities, where a majority of humans currently reside). Little is left to me to add – and nothing to which to object.

You quote Erikson's idea of "'identity confusion' [...] during which socially deviant behavior and/or mental disorders may ensue" – a confusion that results from the adolescent's inability to resolve the crises of the first five of Erikson's stages and therefore lay the foun-dations for constructing "a healthy and stable personal identity". You do it only to ask "does this theory, formulated in the 1970s and based on monocultural societies, assume the same value today, in a time of globalization and complexity?" and then to reply that you don't think so. Well, neither do I. When you quote, with approval, Ulrich Beck's verdict that contemporary *homo complexus,* doomed to be cast in the role of a *homo optionis,* is "condemned to live without certainties and solid points of reference for the formation of values", we agree, again, to accept that verdict. What Erikson could still view as a pathology afflicting a margin of unfortunate failures, has since rose to the level of a norm – or almost. We are now all presumed (some of us rightly, some others counterfactually), instructed and prodded to make our choices and bear responsibility for their anticipated or un-anticipated outcomes. Whether we like it or not, our identities are not given: they are tasks – and tasks that can hardly ever be ultimately completed and wound up. I think that instead of speaking of "identity" – deploying a noun suggestive of a solid entity – we are well advised to speak of the process of "identification" and "re-identification"; in no way straight-lined, but convoluted and all too often contorted, and above all filling the totality of life-span. All and any passed in that process need to be viewed as a snapshot or a half-way inn, a state as under-determined as it is stopping well short of determining its sequels.

Roberto Esposito,[12] a leading Italian political philosopher, unravels the dialectics endemic to the community versus individuality, belonging versus autonomy and constraint versus freedom relationships. While doomed to remain in irresolvable conflict, both sides of each of those oppositions need each other for self-constitution; indeed, each constitutes itself in reference to its adversary. In the case of neighbourhood (a category by and large overlapping with the entity discussed by Esposito under the name of "communitas") the defining factor is the conjunction between the *duty* of giving gifts and the *right* to expect reciprocity. That duty and that right are inseparable from each other. The duty may feel repellent and disabling, unlike the right experienced as welcome and enabling; but one cannot get rid of the duty, however awkward and burdensome, without resigning and losing the right. Hence the inevitable coupling of the attraction and re-pellence of communal membership, as well as of the temptation and fear of the exit (or relegation) from community. "Immunity" resulting from opting out or a banishment is for that reason a blend of blessing and curse. In the rendering of Timothy Campbell, the foremost interpreter of Esposito's teachings,

> immune is he – and immunity is clearly gendered as masculine in the examples from classical Rome that Esposito cites – who is exonerated or has received a dispensation from reciprocal gift-giving. He who has been freed from communal obligations or who enjoys an original autonomy or successive freeing from a previously contracted debt enjoys the

condition of *immunitas*. The relationship immunity maintains with individual identity emerges clearly here. Immunity connotes the means by which the individual is defended from the "expropriative effects" of the community, protecting the one who carries it from the risk of contact with those who do not (the risk being precisely the loss of individual identity).[13]

To cut the long story short: the need/desire of the security of belonging and the need/desire of the freedoms of autonomy being at cross-purposes − complementary and constantly interacting though not easily reconcilable and unlikely to be consumed simultaneously − the life-long identification/re-identification process is a resultant of two countervailing and mutually heteronymous forces. The two needs-desires are locked forever in a tug-of-war, subject to logrolling, shifting to and fro the current (never conclusive, always until-further-notice) resultant. Designing in advance a Sartrean "projet de la vie", let alone sticking to it through thick and thin and following it to the letter, is purely and simply no longer on the cards (if it ever was in practice, not just in imagination). What Siobhan Lyons recently[14] opined, "just as Derrida argues that you can't catch the sea, one can't adequately capture culture while it is still liquid, before it has had time to solidify", applies in equal measure to contemporary identities − forever *in statu nascendi*, in fight for recognition and/or survival, in need of being continually reproduced anew or revised and reformed.

The narrator of Karel Čapek's remarkable novel of a title intimating the author's generalizing intention,[15] tried hard to locate, retrospectively, the inner logic in the apparently contingent and haphazard aggregate of *non-sequitur* sequences in his biography and to reconstruct the forces behind its dynamics. Here are his conclusions:

> Something adjusts itself in man when his life is getting on to its proper line: up till then he has an uncertain possibility of being this, or that, to go here or there, but now it's to be determined by a higher validity that his own will. Therefore his inner self jibs and tosses about, not knowing that these tremors of his are the rattle of the wheels of fate as they run on to the right rail.

Let me explain that the metaphorics deployed in the above narrative (all that jibbing, tossing, rattling, wheels and rails) has been determined as well as justified by its narrator trade of a railway man − implying a crucial, and irremovable role played by the personal, though socially defined life-experience of the synthesizer in her/his (retrospective, let me repeat) attempts at autobiographical synthesis. As Hegel suggested, the calling and fate of philosophy is to attempt to capture its time in an adequate conceptual net. But he also warned (in the introduction to *Philosophy of Right*[16]), that "when philosophy paints its gloomy picture then a form of life has grown old... Only when the dusk starts to fall does the owl of Minerva spread its wings and fly". That iron rule applies to the sense imputed to the story of identities (single or multiple) as much as it does to the history of philosophy. Identities enter biographies (and autobiographies!) in the mode of philosophies entering the narrative of history of philosophy: as postmortems, obituaries and gravestones – rather than as programs, manifestoes and intents or conscious and acted-upon motives.

Identification or re-identification is a process of social interaction: autonomous designs are socially inspired and demanding social recognition. That interaction is enclosed in a social circle known under the name of "neighbourhood", or rather it is precisely that interaction relevant to forming and fixing our identity that we tend to call our neighbourhood: an area inhabited by humans whose approval is a major moving factor, purpose and stake of self-identification processes. Whether a verdict of fate or a product of my own selection and composition, neighbourhood is the territory populated by George Herbert Mead's "significant others"; the space of the confrontation, opposition and reconciliation of the "I" and the "Me"[17] – and the scene on which the dramas of self-identification and the search of recognition are staged.

For the most of human history, and still (by an inertia or by what the anthropologists use to call "cultural lag") in the present day vernacular habits, the idea of a "neighbour" was commonly associated with a person living next door or at least a small distance from where we live. Talking of "neighbourhood", we normally have in mind a relatively small space – walking distance in diameter – populated by people whom we know personally or of whom we know, and who also, probably, know us or at least can be aware of our existence: people most likely to be bumped across whenever we go out, be seen by us in passing on the road to the bus stop, perhaps talked to and with, sometimes to knock to our doors to exchange information or ask for help. "Neighbourhood" is a grey area separating/linking the space of anonymity and that of familiarity. It is also a transit era from the first of those spaces to the second. The news that "someone has moved in to that house up there" triggers the passage.

For the most of human history, the inseparable trait of "neighbours" was our incapacity to select or de-select them. They were, so to speak, a "verdict of fate", facts of the matter − and there was next to nothing one could do change those facts, however strongly one might wish them away. They might move in or out, planting or uprooting themselves in and from neighbourhood on their own (that is, emphatically not ours) initiative and will − we were incapable of make them exit our neighbourhood or keeping them inside against their intentions. They were "just there", given, and however we felt about it, whether we liked it or not, there was little we could do to change it. A variegated lot they tended to be: some seemed nice and pleasant and felt welcome − some other nosy, obtrusive, suspect of ill intention and scheming − or altogether repellent. Our attitudes to such neighbours not of our choice tended to be therefore mixed: we were glad that some of them are in our vicinity, we could endure some others being here, and we would rather get rid of the rest. I repeat: the composition of the neighbourhood was not of our doing. The only choice was to take it or leave it; there was no third option. If you didn't like it, you could move elsewhere (were you able to manage and afford such move) into a different neighbourhood. Once having moved and settled in a neighbourhood and as long as you stayed there, you were, however, a hostage of the fate.

This is not, however, the only way we can draw the line between close and remote, proximity and distance, "in here" and "out there" − indeed, between "us" and "them". We live in the era of time-space compression (a phenomenon first noted and articulated in 1989 by the social geographer David Harvey[18]), in which the correlation between such divisions on one hand and geographical or topographic distances on another has been all but broken. On a planet crisscrossed by information highways and equipped with World-Wide-Web appliances enabling the transmission and reception of information in real time, "neighbourhoods" playing a crucial role in identity formation and reformation need not be, and indeed all-too-often are not, spatially continuous; in their new, electronic version, they can be spatially splintered and dispersed, disseminated and scattered over enormous geographical distances. Under condition of time-space compression, distances from destinations are not measured by miles or kilometres − but by the time required to reach them, and by the grace of the cutting-edge electronic technology, the differences between such times are close to zero. They can be disregarded, or even effaced entirely from the list of factors one needs to consider whenever it comes to determining the degree of inter-human closeness. Thanks to that quality, the electronically composed and sustained "networks" can easily meet electronically the spatial criteria of proximity posited by the orthodox "neighbourhood communities". With one tremendously important proviso, however: unlike the off-line, earthly neighbourhoods in which all its members need to walk through on legs, through electronic neighbourhoods one travels with fingers.

One tremendously important difference between the two varieties of neighbourhood inevitably follows: Cutting out a sort of "domesticated", habituated wedge of relatively well-mapped familiarity out of the vast expanses of unvisited and poorly mapped, unfamiliarized and all too often incomprehensible for that reason off-putting foreigners, an offline, earthly neighbourhood creates *faits accomplis* without asking its residents' permission or consulting with the residents that wedge's dimensions and contents; the electronic neighbourhood dubbed "network" performs the same role and achieves similar results – but by design and under supervision of its owner/manager. It is always somebody's DIY and privately own network, of which its composer and rightful owner who called it into being and continues to sustain while being capable to modify its composition at will, is entitled to say: "I – a personal union of the designer, owner, manager and overseer – am the one who issues or refuses the entry permit – and have power to change my resolution at my desire at pleasure. While being, without having been asked, but one of an undefined number of human objects belonging to an earthly neighbourhood in which I happen to reside at the moment – I am the composer and the central hub of my own electronic neighbourhood; indeed, we are that one cornerstone in its foundation whose withdrawal is bound to cause the collapse of the whole structure and so feel like the Sun around which all others, the planets, rotate. I *belong to* the neighbourhood, whereas the network *belongs to me*: I have selected its members, I have power to establish (and modify at will) the degree of their importance and I assign each of them the role I expect them to play. Willy-nilly, joyfully or gnashing my teeth, I must submit to the explicitly spelled out or unwritten – tacit, albeit keenly observed – rules imposed on the members of an earthly neighbourhood; as for the networks however, it is *I* who articulate the rules to which the members, whether invited or just allowed entry, must submit. I may feel in my neighbourhood at home, but neighbourhood remains nevertheless the realm of the 'must'; depending on the laxity and 'civil inattention' of neighbours, or strictness and obtrusiveness of 'neighbourhood watch', my condition would vary from a few light, innocuous and un-annoying restrictions – all the way to complete loss of privacy. Network, on the other hand, is the territory of unalloyed freedom – at least we would like and expect it to be so". Allow me to sum up all that with the metaphor of coconut-like off-line neighbourhood contrasted with its avocado-like electronic replica.

Networks tempt with the *promise* of immunity from the harsh demands and excruciating quandaries and dilemmas for which the earthly, off-line environments are notorious. Having locked ourselves inside a network, we may even *experience* such immunity. As long as I stay locked as if in an impenetrable cocoon protected by the electronic boundaries of my network easily controlled with my fingers, I may *feel* being genuinely free – not, however, because the constraints, the pressures to conform, and the necessity of facing up to hard choices have all vanished – have been made null and void and lost their coercive power – but because they have been, so to speak, put for a time on a side burner, held at a distance, temporarily suspended: and so blissfully ignored, exiled for a time being from mind and heart. Compared with the discomforts and inconveniences inescapable in the "real" (that is, resistant my attempts of being pushed aside or wished away) neighbourhood, the apparent safety of a network seems to offer a seductive, comfortable shelter. It feels as respite – but does not bring any closer to the resolution the problems that inspired me to seek shelter in the first place. Swept temporarily under the carpet, those problems lose nothing of their venom and are perpetually ready to re-emerge – with a vengeance, and when they do – as they sooner rather than later must – they'd find the escapees yet less equipped to tackle them than they were before the disarmingly tranquil, immobilizingly tranquil sojourn in the electronic refuge from the hurly-burly offline life.

That offline world – the "real" neighbourhood – is in quite a few respects a direct opposite to the online world of the network. Both worlds may be saturated with incertitude – but the uncertainty of the online variety is eminently manageable and reasonably controllable (or so at least it feels), while that of the offline type is blatantly unmanageable and beyond control; for those reasons, the first is the source of enjoyable and gratifyingly effective action and in many, perhaps most cases is experienced as enabling – whereas the second impresses as confused, bewildering and off-putting; for those reasons, it feels disabling.

We – each one of us – live now, intermittently though quite often simultaneously, in two universes: online and offline. The second of the two is frequently dubbed "the real world", though the question whether such label fits it better than does the first turns more debatable by the day.

The two universes differ sharply – by the worldviews they inspire, the skills they require and the behavioural codes they patch together and promote. Their differences can be, and indeed are, negotiated – but hardly reconciled. It is left to every person immersed in both those universes (and that means to all and each of us) to resolve the clashes between them and draw the boundaries of applicability of each one of the two distinct and often mutually contradictory codes. But the experience derived from one universe cannot but affect the way in which we view the other universe, evaluate it and move through; there tends to be a constant, legal or illegal but always heavy, border traffic between the two universes.

Notes

1 E. H. Erikson, *Childhood and Society* (New York: Norton & Comp., 1963); E.H. Erikson, *Identity, Youth and Crisis* (New York: Norton & Comp., 1968).

2 Erikson, *Childhood and Society* (New York: Norton & Comp., 1963), pp. 231–258; Erikson, *Identity, Youth and Crisis* (New York: Norton & Comp., 1968), pp. 107–166.

3 cf. Erikson, *Identity, Youth and Crisis* (New York: Norton & Comp., 1968), pp. 167–246.

4 U. Beck, *Risikogesellschaft: Auf demWeg in eine andere Moderne* (Frankfurt am Main: Surkamp, 1986).

5 Z. Bauman, *In Search of Politics* (Cambridge: Polity Press, 1999).

6 Ibid., p. 64.

7 Z. Bauman, *Intervista sull'identità (Interview on Identity)* (Roma-Bari: Laterza, 2003).

8 Ibid., p. 29.

9 A. Portera, *Interkulturelle Identitäten* (Köln: Böhlau, 1995); A. Portera, "Identity Development in a Multicultural Context: Risks and Educational Opportunities," *European Journal of Intercultural Studies* 8, no. 3, 1997, pp. 247–256; A. Portera, *Tesori sommersi. Emigrazione, identità, bisogni educativi interculturali* (Milano: FrancoAngeli, 2014) (1st ed. 1997).

10 Based on the main research's results, considering also other studies and theories – like Maslow, *Motivation and Personality* (New York: Harper & Row Publishers, 1954), Rogers, *On Personal Power: Inner Strength and Its Revolutionary Impact* (New York: Delacorte Press, 1977, 1987) and Erikson (1968) – I developed a theory of fundamental needs of human development, which complete or partial satisfaction seems to be correlated with the manifestation of conflicts, disturbances or illness. Above all, migration and life in a multicultural context seems to limit the fulfillment of the following needs: for social relations and for belonging; for bonding; for deep understanding (empathy); for active participation; for continuity.

11 J. Derrida, *Cosmopolites de tous les Pays* (Paris: Editions Galilée, 1997).

12 R. Esposito, *The Origin and Destiny of Community,* trans. Timothy Campbell (Redwood City: Stanford UP, 2009).

13 See Timothy Campbell, "Bíos, Immunity, Life: The Thought of Roberto Esposito". http://www.biopolitica.unsw.edu.au/sites/all/files/publication_related_files/campbell_introduction_bios.pdf

14 Siobhan Lyons, "Alternatives of Modernism", *Philosophy Now*, June–July 2015.
15 *An Ordinary Life,* here quoted in M. and R. Wetheralls' English translation (North Haven: Catbird Press, 1900), p. 364.
16 G. W. F. Hegel, *Philosophy of Right* (New York: Galaxy Books, 1968), p. 12.
17 George Herbert Mead, *Mind, Self, and Society* (Chicago: University of Chicago Press, 1934).
18 In David Harvey, *The Condition of Postmodernity: An Enquiry into the Origins of Cultural Change* (Oxford: Blackwell, 1990).

Part III

Conclusions

Conclusions

Agostino Portera

In the above conversation, we stated the challenges related with globalization, religious pluralism, and identity building in a pluralistic, multicultural society, as well as several risks: above all pollution, neoliberalism and establishing bureaucratic societies which privilege process, order and efficiency over morals, responsibility and care for the other. As a result, there is a growing disorientation regarding rules, values and modes of interaction: decreasing of stable bonds and of the ability to cope with conflicts, frustration and stress. Today, where only making money, audience, speed and technology seem to count, human beings are becoming more and more dominated, alone and unable to communicate. As expressed above, at the present time, there is an extreme need for community, for citizens in democratic societies that are able to be self-critical, responsible and able to pursue the common good. The problem that we face is determining how we can rebuild stable and robust human structures, rebuild common humanity and overcome all the barriers that divide, instead of including, and often position humans as enemies, one against the other. Given the mentioned problems and the disastrous ecologic situation, the question is not if we can or will integrate some foreign persons: *The human species is at risk of going extinct*, and, as Bauman best expressed above, "there are little (or at least far too few) signs that are given the attention which their import and gravity require". Also the few Cassandra's voices remain always unheeded. So as the Trojan War took place, our generation today asks our fathers how could things happen like the catastrophic World Wars, the deportation and the best organized extermination of "different" human beings (Jewish, Roma, homosexual, politically different). Tomorrow our children will be asking us why we did not intervene in stopping the above-mentioned actions of mistreatment and calamities. We are not just spectators; we are participants and have a piece of the responsibility. The fact of the matter is that, in this world, as humans "We're all in the same boat; a hole at one end will sink us all".[1] Either we'll save collectively or we'll perish together. *Tertium non datur.*

A possible way to solve some of the aforementioned problems was identified: *education.* For overcoming the crisis in Greece, Socrates stated the need for politics (as a form of organization and government) and education: "Athens needs good politicians, which need to be well educated".[2] After 2,000 years, nowadays it is still necessary to invest more in education, in all forms and places: starting with the family, continuing in school and extending in the workplace, politics, public sphere and mass media. Unlike animals, the human person needs education to unpack his/her best potential and also for learning to take care of oneself, of other living beings and of the environment. Today, *intercultural education* could be considered to be the best developed model. It is located between universalism and relativism, based on the advantages of transcultural education (education to common humanities, human rights, human ethics and human needs) and multicultural education (education to acknowledge and respect other persons and cultures), yet in addition there is the opportunity of interaction: encounter, dialogue, confront, conflict management. Next to education, in order to govern diversity, in all areas of human existence there is also an urgent necessity to assume *Intercultural Competences,* for recognizing opportunities and risks of the new situation, and for facing the inevitable conflicts related with the increasing mobility, interdependence, and cultural complexity. The intercultural approach allows people to act in the best form of education and teaching. Intercultural competencies present an intervention which takes into account and deals with *all manners of diversity,* not only linguistic, cultural, or somatic, but also, for instance, gender, political, social status or economic differences. In short, in the 21st century we need intercultural *formae mentis* in all sectors of our life, and also in the relationship with ourselves.

Zygmunt Bauman died on 9 January 2017, aged 91. As M. Davis and T. Campbell[3] best evoked, his metaphor of the *liquid modernity,* which analysed the loss of the solid structures and described the foundations for contemporary societies, and the consequences for individuals and communities, made him famous not just for the anti-globalization movement, but also for many scholars, teachers and citizens around the world. His reflections were based not only on theories and the many publications that he deeply analyzed, but also on the experiences as protagonist among young activists in Spain, Italy and across Central and South America, and also on his experiences of poverty, marginalization and exile (he was twice a refugee). His motto was: "See the world through the eyes of society's weakest members, and then tell anyone honestly that our societies are good, civilised, advanced, free". As was partially evident above, Bauman declined to suggest concrete solutions to the many chances and risks. However, also in his publications it is clear that he believed in a form of socialism that shows constant attention to every citizen (especially the weakest), in which people could overcome the status of individualized consumers, by finding solutions to their private concerns by shopping: "Can notions of equality, democracy and self-determination survive when society is seen less and less as a product of shared labour and common values and far more as a mere container of goods and services to be grabbed by competing individual hands?".[4] He supported societies in which persons share common public issues, and where everyone can act collectively as citizens. As Davis and Campbell further underline, Bauman "believed ardently that the European Union stood as a safeguard for hard-won rights and for shared protection against war and social insecurity". Therefore "his work serves as a reminder that our world has been made by human hands and so it can be remade by them too. For all his passion and pessimism, he wrote because he believed that that challenge could and should be confronted".

For me, having had the opportunity to meet him, work with him and also write this book together, is a great honour and privilege. As we share the same birthday (however, just the day and month, not the year), I feel in some way obliged to persist in his footsteps. Perhaps the best way is by trying to reflect on an adequate form of intervention for revising our world as a better place to live for every animate and inanimate being. In this book, but also in the previous one written with R. Mazzeo,[5] Bauman clearly asserts his trust in education as a way for humans to remake our world so that it can be better for all humans, animals, plants and all other forms of existence.

Bauman's long and fruitful life, and also his death, offers us many further impulses for reflections. What is the scope of life? What happens after death? In Confucianism, but also in Taoism and Buddhism, the word *Tao,* means the "right way". Our life is regulated with two poles: *yin* (darkness, shadow, passivity) and *yang* (light, activity). In this idea, unlike many other religions, there is not a metaphysical dualism: life-principle, sexuality, heaven and earth are part of a unity. Life is generated by the bi-polar tension. At the moment of conception, there is a division between the heart as place for emotional consciousness (*hsin*) and logos (*hsing*). In the course of existence, living humans form two parts: the *animus* is bright and active and dwells in the eyes, and the *anima,* situated in the abdomen, is dark and earth-bound. After death, the *anima* sinks to the earth and decays; the *animus* rises in the air (as higher soul), where first it is active and then evaporates in ethereal space, or in the reservoir of life.[6] I believe that today we can take many important impulses from this thousands of years old *Weltanschauung.* First, life (*ming*) is always super individual to understand. As animate and inanimate creatures in this world, we are all deeply connected and are constantly dependent upon one another. Then, it is not possible to distinguish between good and evil (right or wrong, health or ill, similar or foreigners, aggressive and passive persons). Life is a result of tension between day and night, passivity and activity, water and fire, masculine and feminine. Perfection, or the secret of life, is not to follow and develop just one of these poles. Instead, similar to the intercultural approach, it is to reach in the dynamic flow, as an inner, ascending circulation and mastering of the forces originating from *anima* and *animus, yin* and *yang,* logos and emotion. Therefore, it is important to remain flexible, to learn how to interact best with others and within our self. In this regard, the Tao teaches: "Men [and women] are born soft and supple; dead, they are stiff and hard. Plants are born tender and pliant; dead, they are brittle and dry",[7] and further "Nothing in the world is as soft and yielding as water. Yet for dissolving the hard and inflexible, nothing can surpass it. The soft overcomes the hard; the gentle overcomes the rigid".[8] Therefore, as intercultural education also intends, the secret of good life is to become and remain like water, soft and yielding, and avoid getting hard, stiff and inflexible.

In his commentary to the above book, C.G. Jung warns us that "he [human] is not the only master in his house".[9] Next to *anima* and *animus, yin* and *yang, hsin and hsing,* in us the unconscious also lives. The house, and also the world in which we are living are really plenty populated. We cannot avoid it, as diversity and variety are the fundamental principle of our life. Our species as *homo sapiens sapiens* has survived not because of violence, oppression or power (dinosaurs did it much longer and better). The challenge today is to learn to live together as equals, respecting all diversities, building cooperative communities and taking care of each other, especially society's weakest members. Education is a necessary step in this direction.

Notes

1 Kofi Annan, "Kofi Annan's Speech to the General Assembly 13 September 2002," *The Guardian,* December 10, 2009.

2 D. R. Morrison, *The Cambridge Companion to Socrates* (Cambridge: Cambridge University Press, 2010).
3 M. Davis and T. Campbell, *The Guardian*, January 15, 2017.
4 Ibid.
5 Z. Bauman and R. Mazzeo, *On Education* (Cambridge: Polity Press, 2012).
6 R. Wilhelm, *The Secret of the Golden Flower* (New York: Harcout, 1932), pp. 13–15.
7 Lau Tzu, *Tao the Ching* (London: Frances Lincoln, 1999), nr. 76.
8 Ibid., nr. 78.
9 R. Wilhelm, "C. G. Jung Commentary", in *The Secret of the Golden Flower* (New York: Harcout, 1932), p. 112.

References

Arpaia B., *Qualcosa là fuori (Something Out There)* (Parma: Guanda, 2016).

Bandura A., *Moral Disengagement. How People Do Harm and Live With Themselves* (New York: Worth Publishers, 2016).

Bauman Z., *In Search of Politics* (Cambridge: Polity Press, 1999).

Bauman Z., *Society Under Siege* (Cambridge: Polity Press, 2002).

Bauman Z., *Liquid Love: On the Frailty of Human Bonds* (Cambridge: Polity Press, 2003a).

Bauman Z., *Intervista sull'identità (Interview on Identity)*, ed. Benedetto Vecchi (Bari-Rome and Cambridge: Laterza and Polity Press, 2003b).

Bauman Z., *Liquid Modernity* (Cambridge: Polity Press, 2000, 2012).

Bauman Z., "Liquid Modern Challenges to Education", in *Intercultural Education and Competences: Challenges and Answers for the Global World*. eds. A. Portera, C. A. Grant (Newcastle: Cambridge Scholars, 2016).

Bauman Z., Heller Á., *La bellezza (non) ci salverà* (Trento: Il Margine, 2015).

Bauman Z., Mazzeo R., *On Education* (Cambridge: Polity Press, 2012).

Bauman Z., Mazzeo R., *In Praise of Literature* (Cambridge: Polity Press, 2016).

Bauman Z., Obirek S., *Conversazioni su Dio e sull'uomo* (Roma-Bari: Laterza, 2014).

Beck U., *Risikogesellschaft: Auf dem Weg in eine andere Moderne* (Frankfurt am Main: Surkamp, 1986).

Bertman S., *Hyperculture: The Human Cost of Speed* (Santa Barbara: Praeger, 1998).

Brennan T., *Exhausting Modernity: Grounds for a New Economy* (New York: Routledge, 2000).

Campbell, T. "Bíos, Immunity, Life: The Thought of Roberto Esposito." http://www.biopolitica.unsw.edu.au/sites/all/files/publication_related_files/ campbell_introduction_bios.pdf.

Cavalli Sforza L. F., *Chi siamo. La storia della diversità umana* (Milano: Mondadori, 1993).

Derrida J., *Cosmopolites de tous les Pays* (Paris: Editions Galilée, 1997).

Erikson E. H., *Childhood and Society* (New York: Norton & Comp., 1963).

Erikson E. H., *Identity, Youth and Crisis* (New York: Norton & Comp., 1968).

Esposito R., *The Origin and Destiny of Community*, trans. T. Campbell (Redwood City: Stanford UP, 2009).

Fish S., "Boutique Multiculturalism, or Why Liberals Are Incapable of Thinking about Hate Speech", *Critical Inquiry* 23, no. 2 (Winter 1997), pp. 378–395.

Fish S., *The Problem with Principle* (Cambridge: Harvard UP, 1999).

Harvey D., *The Condition of Postmodernity: An Enquiry into the Origins of Cultural Change* (Oxford: Blackwell, 1990).

Heller Á., Mazzeo R., *Wind and Whirlwind: Utopian and Dystopian Themes in Literature and Philosophy* (Leiden/Boston: Brill, 2019).

Klein N., *This Changes Everything: Capitalism vs. the Climate* (London: Allen Lane, 2014).

Lau Tzu, *Tao the Ching* (London: Frances Lincoln, 1999).

Lewontin R., *La diversité génétique humaine* (Paris: Puf, 1984).

Magatti M., *Oltre l'infinito. Storia della potenza dal sacro alla tecnica* (Milan: Feltrinelli, 2018).

Mead G. H., *Mind, Self, and Society* (Chicago: University of Chicago Press, 1934).

Molari C., *Teologia del pluralismo religioso (Theology of Religious Pluralism)* (Rome: Pazzini, 2012).

Morrison D. R., *The Cambridge Companion to Socrates* (Cambridge: Cambridge University Press, 2010).

Portera A., *Europei senza Europa. Storia e storie di vita di giovani italiani in Germania* (Catania: Coesse, 1990).

Portera A., *Interkulturelle Identitäten* (Köln: Böhlau, 1995).

Portera A., "Identity Development in a Multicultural Context: Risks and Educational Opportunities", *European Journal of Intercultural Studies* 8, no. 3 (1997), pp. 247–256.

Portera A., The Religious Education in a Pluralistic and Multicultural Society", in *Self-investigation and Transcendence. Psychological Approaches to the Religious Identity in a Pluralistic Society*, eds. M. Aletti, G. Rossi (Turin: Centro Scientifico Editore, 1999), pp. 317–324.

Portera A., "Multicultural and Intercultural Education in Europe", in *Intercultural and Multicultural Education: Enhancing Global Interconnectedness*, eds. C. A. Grant, A. Portera (New York: Routledge, 2011), pp. 12–32.

Portera A., *Manuale di pedagogia interculturale* (Roma-Bari: Laterza, 2013).

Portera A., *Tesori sommersi. Emigrazione, identità, bisogni educativi interculturali* (Milan: FrancoAngeli, 2014) (1st ed., 1997).

Rabhi P., *Manifeste pour la Terre e pour l'Humanisme* (Arles: Actes Sud, 2008).

Ramadan T., Mazzeo R., *Il musulmano e l'agnostico* (Trento: Erickson, 2016).

Rovelli C., *La realtà non è ciò che appare (Reality is Not What it Seems)* (Milan: Raffaello Cortina, 2014).

Schwarzenbach R. P., Gschewend P. M., Imboden D. M., *Environmental Organic Chemistry* (New York: Wiley, 2003).

Seinfeld J. H., Pandies S. N., *Atmospheric Chemistry and Physics: From Air Pollution to Climate Change* (New York: Wiley 1998).

Smolin L., *Time Reborn* (Turin: Einaudi, 2014).

Soros G., *The Crisis of Global Capitalism* (New York: Perseus Books, 1998).

Tortello L., "Bauman Talks of God but Doesn't Know if it Exists" *La Stampa*, September 24, 2014.

West B. A., *Encyclopedia of the Peoples of Asia and Oceania* (New York: Infobase Publishing, 2008).

Wilhelm R., *The Secret of the Golden Flower* (New York: Harcourt, 1932).

Wilson E. O., *The Creation: An Appeal to Save Life on Earth* (New York: W.W. Norton & Company, 2006).

Index